PRAISE FOR
Penelope J. Stokes

"Penelope Stokes is a bright beacon. Her stories touch the heart, engage the brain, and expand the spirit."

—Philip Gulley, author of the Harmony series

"With abiding warmth and moving sensitivity, Stokes crafts an inspiring tribute to the power of true friendship." —*Booklist*

"A beautiful novel of dreams gone awry . . . speaks to the truths of our connection to the universe and to who we really are."

—Joan Medlicott, author of *Promises of Change*

"You'll want to buy several copies of this book, one to keep for yourself, the others to give to the women friends you are fortunate enough to include in your circle of grace."

—Lynne Hinton, author of *The Order of Things* and *Friendship Cake*

"Stokes has an unquenchable penchant for using the symbolism of objects as a springboard for her stories . . . Her prose is smooth as butter." —*Publishers Weekly*

The Book of Peach

PENELOPE J. STOKES

BERKLEY BOOKS, NEW YORK

THE BERKLEY PUBLISHING GROUP
Published by the Penguin Group
Penguin Group (USA) Inc.
375 Hudson Street, New York, New York 10014, USA
Penguin Group (Canada), 90 Eglinton Avenue East, Suite 700, Toronto, Ontario M4P 2Y3, Canada
(a division of Pearson Penguin Canada Inc.)
Penguin Books Ltd., 80 Strand, London WC2R 0RL, England
Penguin Group Ireland, 25 St. Stephen's Green, Dublin 2, Ireland (a division of Penguin Books Ltd.)
Penguin Group (Australia), 250 Camberwell Road, Camberwell, Victoria 3124, Australia
(a division of Pearson Australia Group Pty. Ltd.)
Penguin Books India Pvt. Ltd., 11 Community Centre, Panchsheel Park, New Delhi—110 017, India
Penguin Group (NZ), 67 Apollo Drive, Rosedale, North Shore 0632, New Zealand
(a division of Pearson New Zealand Ltd.)
Penguin Books (South Africa) (Pty.) Ltd., 24 Sturdee Avenue, Rosebank, Johannesburg 2196,
South Africa

Penguin Books Ltd., Registered Offices: 80 Strand, London WC2R 0RL, England

This book is an original publication of The Berkley Publishing Group.

PRINTING HISTORY
Berkley trade paperback edition / August 2010

Library of Congress Cataloging-in-Publication Data

Stokes, Penelope J.
    The book of Peach : a novel / Penelope J. Stokes.—Berkley trade paperback ed.
        p. cm.
    ISBN 978-0-425-23449-5
    1. Self-realization in women—Fiction. 2. Chick lit. I. Title.
    PS3569.T6219B66 2010
    813'.54—dc22
                                    2010006128

PRINTED IN THE UNITED STATES OF AMERICA

10   9   8   7   6   5   4   3   2   1

For Pam,
now and always

Acknowledgments

Special thanks to my agent, Claudia Cross, and my editor, Wendy McCurdy, for their ongoing support and encouragement.

And to my family of choice, my family of faith, all the people in my life who love and support me in the valleys and on the mountains. You know who you are. Thank you.

Thou art thy mother's glass, and she in thee

Calls back the lovely April of her prime.

WILLIAM SHAKESPEARE

Preamble

Make no mistake; I was brought up to be a Southern Lady. Not a Southern *girl*, mind you. Southern girls are an accident of birth and geography. Southern Ladies are an intentional crafting, shaped in their malleable years until they are perfectly sculpted and flawless, ready to harden.

Contrary to popular opinion and Hollywood images, everyone in the South knows that wealth is not the primary issue in becoming a Southern Lady. Nor is beauty. Nor are character, integrity, honor, grace, charm, or any of the other virtues Southerners claim to revere.

What's important is the Name.

A girl can be ugly as a mud fence and dumb as a brick, not to mention crafty as a cockroach, but if she has the right name and the right heritage, she can get by just fine.

She will marry well, wear designer clothes, carry a gold card, and be recognized at a hundred yards by every waiter at the country club.

She will, in short, become a Southern Lady.

It's all in the Name.

In the beginning, Adam was given the task of naming all the animals of creation. But before he even knew what hit him, Eve took over the job, and women have held the post ever since. Naming has been refined through the eons, since our First Mother pondered a giraffe, but it is nevertheless a heritage still closely guarded and maintained by the mothers of would-be Southern Ladies.

I grew up in Mississippi, in an obscure little town called Chulahatchie, on the banks of the Tombigbee River. As Mama is quick to remind me, however, I am not a child of Mississippi. My gilded lineage traces back several generations to a remote branch of the Bell family, one of Tennessee's finest, from up around Clarksville.

By the time the Late Unpleasantness was over and the carpetbaggers had feasted on the spoils of war, the Bells no longer had two nickels to rub together or a pot to piss in. But they did have a couple of assets that enabled them to hold on to their place in society: a good name and an ancestral home.

The good name, of course, had nothing to do with honor or integrity, and by the turn of the new century, the ancestral home was falling down around the Bells' patrician heads. But still they held the land, and still they held out hope for future generations. Hope in the form of the Name that would be passed on. The family Name, the bedrock, the mortar that binds together the disparate stones of crumbling Southern culture.

Because my Bell heritage came through my mother's side of the family, the Name could easily have been lost to the ravages of time and social custom. Southern women do, after all, adhere to the old-fashioned notion of women taking their husbands' names at the altar. But the Bell women weren't about to lose their connection to the Bell line. If they couldn't keep the Name when they married, by God, they would hang on to it elsewhere.

The female trunk of the family tree, then, went something like this: My grandmother GiGi, Mama's mama, carried the name Georgia Bell Posner Barclay. Mama was Donna Bell Barclay Rondell. My older sister, who was thirteen and humiliated when I was born, was christened Melanie Bell Barclay Rondell. And I, with infant tongue unable to protest, was saddled with Priscilla Bell Posner Rondell.

Peach, to my friends and most of my family.

Mama, of course, refused to acknowledge this nickname and *always* called me Priscilla. Or if she was really angry, "Priscilla Bell!" To this day it gets my attention. I was a Bell, my mother would remind me when I got out of line, and I had better learn to act like one.

It was rumored—and my family fed the supposition and blew upon its dying embers, I suspect—that my ancestors traced back to the original Tennessee Bells, hosts and victims of the famous Bell Witch. All during my childhood and youth I heard stories of the Bell Witch, tales designed to instill in me a healthy respect for my foremothers and a reverence for the Name that had been handed down to me. My warped, rebellious little psyche had great fun with the concept. For years I entertained myself with the assertion that all "belles" were witches, and of course my own mother confirmed that belief at every turn. Once I learned the forbidden word, I played with puns inside my mind: *belle + witch = bitch.*

I knew that "bitch" was an ugly word, not a word that a Southern Lady would use—in polite company or anywhere else—and so it delighted me all the more. For hours, as I practiced before a full-length mirror learning to "carry myself," I would mouth the word over and over under my breath: bitch, bitch, bitch. I said it behind my mother's back when she corrected my posture, and I repeated it as a silent incantation to block out the incessant lectures on what was and was not appropriate behavior for a Southern Lady. She never caught me, not even when I said it over her head as she was hemming my gown for the Miss Mississippi Pageant.

It was an invisible victory, a tiny hairline fissure in the plaster of my mold. But it was a beginning. A harbinger of things to come.

The day after my graduation from college, I shook the red clay of Mississippi off my pumps and vowed never to return again.

That was twenty-three years ago.

Now, God help me, I'm back.

PART ONE

Backstory

. . .

Erasing
rubs the words away
but still the imprint
on the page
remains.
Unlearning
is the hardest lesson
of them all.

· 1 ·

It's all my psychiatrist's fault.

The turning point came the week I turned forty-five. One Friday evening in October I celebrated my birthday with my husband, Robert; my best friend, Julia; and her current boyfriend, Kenneth. It was one of those magical autumn evenings in Asheville—a glorious pink and purple sunset over the western mountains, followed by a diamond-studded dark blue night sky and a crescent of silver moon. Champagne and candlelight at the Grove Park Inn, dinner on the Sunset Terrace, music on the crisp, cool air. Perfect.

The following Monday afternoon, while I was at the Grove Park Spa getting a massage with the gift certificate Julia had given me as a birthday present, Robert left a voice mail informing me that he had fallen out of love with me and into love with someone else.

Ironically, it was the birthday that hit me hardest—harder even than Robert's abrupt and unexpected departure. At forty, I could still claim to be closer to my thirties than my fifties. Even at forty-four, I hadn't quite crested the hill.

But when I turned forty-five, I suddenly found myself standing on the dizzying precipice of middle age, looking down the dark valley of dotage. One short slide away from being a bona fide dowager. A crone.

What's more, when I glanced back over my shoulder, I saw precious few mountaintops gilded by sunlight. Mostly just a maze of aimless paths and dead ends and quite a number of smoldering ruins, most recent among them the demise of my twenty-year marriage.

It took me all fall and winter and into the early spring to come to these insights. In late February I finally made the mistake of confessing my self-doubt to my therapist.

I sobbed and sniffed and told him everything. "I don't know what I'm going to do," I said. "I've run out of money. Robert's going to take over the house because I can't afford to keep it. I've got no place to go, no job, no prospects. I'm forty-five years old, and I have no options."

"There are always options," the old fool said. "Always choices." He peered at me with bright beady eyes over a hawkish nose. "The past both informs and transforms the future. Maybe you could spend some time at home.

A month or two—or more, if you're so inclined. Get your feet under you. Decide what you'd like to do with your life. Revisit certain issues in the way you were raised."

My head snapped up. "Raised?" I said. "Cows are raised. Cabbages are raised. Southern Ladies are *brought up*."

Holy shit, I thought. *I'm channeling my mother.*

He leaned forward and laid a bony claw on the arm of my chair. "Sometimes we discover where we're going only by finding out where we've come from," he said. "Go home. Talk to her. She's in that big house all alone; surely she'd welcome an extended visit from her daughter." He grinned, showing crooked white teeth. "Besides, you've always dreamed of becoming a writer. Consider it research. Keep a journal. Listen to your soul."

A journal. A record of my life, of my relationship with Mama, of my feelings about Robert's rejection, of the downward spirals and abysmal failures that brought me to this place. A fearless, gutsy, unedited confrontation of myself. An attempt to squeeze insight from experience and find a way back to my center.

Terrifying. Utterly terrifying.

Therapy is no stroll in the park, or even a precarious climb up a raveling rope ladder. It is free-scaling. Finding hand- and toeholds in the smallest of seams, hanging on for dear life, and reminding yourself with every grueling inch that you can neither stay put nor go back down again. No climbing gear, no safety hooks, no rappelling ropes. No tether. Just you and the mountain, and some white-haired old fool on the ground below bellowing encouragements into the shifting wind.

This is not a journey for the faint of heart. It takes a stalwart soul to look into one's dark places and bring the light. I've encountered, in dreams and nightmares and even when I'm wide awake, things that would make space aliens and monsters seem tame by comparison. I've battled them, these fire-breathers that wake after sundown. I've done my best, only to find myself retreating from the fray with eyebrows singed.

And now he is sending me back into the dragon's lair.

To my mother's house.

Lord, how I hate being a stereotype.

· 2 ·

Mama's house—the house Daddy bought and restored for her—was a six-thousand-square-foot Greek Revival mansion, built of slave-made red brick with a wide front verandah and six huge square columns. The original plantation, once called the Mabry Estate, had spread out for a thousand acres on both sides of the river.

Most of the land had long since been sold and the slave quarters razed. Now the town of Chulahatchie encroached upon the place like kudzu, and all that remained of the old plantation was the big house, the small brick kitchen, and the carriage house. Perched on a bank above the river, the home lay surrounded by four acres of lush greenery and a wide driveway flanked by a gauntlet of ancient live oak trees draped in Spanish moss.

In a brilliant turn of wit, Daddy had punned off Mama's name and dubbed the place Belladonna.

She thought it was a tribute to her, his "beautiful lady." I suspect that what he really had in mind was deadly night-shade. Poison of choice for the ancients.

Daddy.

The thought of him raised a lump in my throat the size of a grapefruit. The last time I'd been home was for his funeral a year ago in January, and before that, only a handful of times in the twenty-some years Robert and I were married.

My brother and sister came to the funeral, too, bound by filial duty but dragging their heels in the dust. Harry, as always, remained aloof and untouchable. Melanie curled in upon herself with the pain of the loss of Daddy. I moved numbly through the visitation and funeral, vaguely aware of townspeople coming and going but never seeing their faces or hearing the words of consolation that were spoken. All I remember was Daddy lying in the open coffin, his face waxy and pale, with two spots of mortician's rouge on his cheeks, to make him look "lifelike."

Standing there looking down at him, I felt the weight of a thousand regrets, a thousand questions, a thousand sorrows. It had never occurred to me to wonder what my father's life with my mother had been like—whether he truly loved her, and why. Whether, when they were alone, they ever laughed together, or wept, or touched. Whether he understood why the children he adored had left home and rarely returned even for the briefest of visits.

Now he was gone, and the sweeping entry to Belladonna suddenly looked shriveled and empty and forlorn.

All my life, I never caught my mother unawares. Whenever I came home from wherever I had been—an afternoon of shopping, my senior prom, my first spring break during my freshman year in college—she seemed to know instinctively the exact moment of my arrival. How she did it will forever remain a mystery, but even now, after all these years, I turned in the driveway and she was already on the porch, waving a handkerchief in my direction. For a moment, as I paused between the first two oaks and caught a glimpse of her in the distance, I had a flashback to the dollhouse that took up a quarter of my bedroom when I was a child. A miniature of Belladonna, complete with a little Mama doll in a blue shirtwaist and matching low-heeled pumps.

She looked so tiny. But I was the one who was shrinking. I could feel the regression: forty-five to thirty-five . . . twenty . . . fifteen . . . ten . . . five. The veiled oaks marched by and the years fell away. By the time I pulled the car to a stop at the curve that went around to the carriage house, I was a child again, and my mother, all five-foot-two of her, towered over me.

"Hello, dahlin'," she called from the top step. "Thank goodness you're here!"

I waited for the guilt and was not disappointed. "It's been so *long*." She surveyed me up and down with her icy blue eyes, taking in the jeans, the cotton sweater, the tennis shoes. "Well, I'm sure you've brought other clothes with you, haven't you? Come on in. I expected you an hour ago; I've been beside myself."

Hot damn, I thought. *Now there's two of you.*

"Put your things away," Mama said, "and I'll meet you on the back verandah."

The back verandah. A euphemism, to be sure.

Belladonna is one of those Southern plantation homes that has no back, but rather, two fronts: one facing the street and one facing the river. It's a metaphor of life with Mama. God forbid we should fail to offer a presentable image, even to our own backsides.

Behind the house, past the brick kitchen where slave women once cooked greens and field peas and rutabaga and corn bread for the white residents of the Big House, the lawn sloped down through manicured beds of azalea bushes to the river bluff. The house sat up high, well above flood stage, with a clear view of the lazy brown waters of the Tombigbee.

Mama served lemonade and cookies on the back verandah, and we made small talk, commenting on how the azaleas were budding and would be in full bloom in a week or so and how the redbuds were already coming out. A weeping cherry tree trailed its branches across the lawn, shedding petals like pale pink snow. Along the walkway, in perfect symmetry, stood a line of bright forsythia nodding their yellow dreadlocks in the morning sun.

She didn't say one word about Daddy. I didn't say one word about Robert. At last she set down her glass and fixed her eyes on a point just to the left of my shoulder. "And how long, exactly, am I to have the pleasure of my daughter's company?" she asked.

I wondered vaguely how she managed, in one brief question, to communicate guilt over my absence and annoyance at my presence all in the same breath. But I didn't linger too long over the dilemma. "I don't know," I said. "Are you on a schedule?"

She gave me a chilly smile. "Of course not. I was just curious, that's all. You know you're always welcome here, whenever you need a place to stay. This is your *home*, after all."

Belladonna hadn't been my home in over two decades, but what purpose would it serve to point that out?

We lapsed into silence. A family of chittering squirrels chased each other up and down the big pecan tree, and out on the river two black men caught a fish and annoyed my mother by laughing too loudly.

They were anchored right off our bluff, with the prow of the little green boat pointing downstream. Mama didn't say anything. The river was public, and she couldn't control who drifted by, but she never had to say a word to express her displeasure. All she needed was *the look*.

I'd learned *the look* early in life and took pains to avoid it at all costs. Unsuccessfully, I might add. No matter what I did, no matter how hard I tried, I could never quite manage to do things right. To *be* right. Years ago I had thrown up my hands in despair and said the hell with it, but all the resolutions in kingdom come can't begin to hold back the drowning tide of maternal disapproval.

Now I felt it again, that sensation of traveling back in time, regressing. I lurched backward forty years and saw *the look* in my mother's eyes.

She reached out, plucked at the leg of my blue jeans, and sighed. Just a sigh. That was all. But that sigh, and the silence that followed, carried the reprimand of a lifetime: *For God's sake, Priscilla, learn to be a lady. I brought you up better than this.*

Down on the river, the black men laughed again.

• 3 •

My mother's primary goal in life was to "bring me up right." To that end, she threw herself zealously into the task of molding my young clay into the form of Southern Lady–hood.

My earliest memory of the process of upbringing occurred when I was, perhaps, eighteen months old.

Psychologists—including the white-haired old fool who sent me home again—have repeatedly told me that a child that young is not capable of formulating coherent memories. But the image is seared in my mind, nevertheless. Therapists don't know everything, and besides, I was a very bright child.

I paused, looked down at the journal, reread what I'd

written, and smiled. So there. The old fool wanted me to explore my past, fine. He asked for it; he deserved whatever he got.

And so what if it came across just a tad egotistical? I *was* a very bright child. And I *do* have those memories, no matter what anyone else might argue.

My mother, a petite, perfectly dressed woman with no maternal instincts whatsoever, was attempting to feed me strained spinach from a Gerber jar. The silver spoon wavered for just an instant, and my tiny fist sent it flying, most of it into my mother's hair, the rest with a resounding splat onto the wall behind her head. I pointed a fat baby finger and did the unthinkable: I laughed.

"Priscilla," Mama reprimanded, trying to maintain her dignity with spinach all over her coiffure, "proper young ladies do not throw their food. They eat what is set before them, whether they like it or not."

I responded, or so my father told me, by spitting up the remains of the spinach and using it as fingerpaint on the tray of my high chair. Even at that tender age I was given to the artistic.

All right, maybe I don't remember it—at least not the exact dialogue. I will say in my own defense that I have a vivid recollection of a green stain on the wall to the left of my high chair, at just about the height of my mother's head. Besides, the story gives me pleasure, and so I tell it as truth.

Lord, that sounds just like something Daddy would have said. "Never let the truth get in the way of a good story."

Except I think it's more accurate to say, "Never let reality get in the way of a good story." Nothing tells the truth quite so precisely as good fiction. It's reality that bogs down the process.

Maybe that's a working principle for this journal of mine—not to get caught in the tangle of details, how this happened or what exact words were said. What's important here is the insight I'm supposed to get from returning to the scene of the crime and revisiting those old memories and feelings and experiences. So I'll just spin it out as it comes to me and see what gets caught in the web.

I learned fiction from my father—a storyteller of renown among our friends and relatives. Daddy called it entertaining. Mama called it by another name. I came to dread the expression on her face every time he launched into one of his elaborate tales. Clearly, she was not amused. Not one bit.

By the time I was four or five, Daddy was already being eased out of any involvement in my upbringing. To my mother, "bringing me up right" meant instilling in me the social graces, the values and priorities that accompanied the Bell name.

My basic nature did not cooperate with the agenda. At four I learned to read, teaching myself with my older brother's first-grade primers and my collection of fairy tales and children's poems. At four and a half, I determined that I wanted to be a writer. I was captivated by the magic and mystery of words, how little black squiggles on a white page could conjure up dream worlds and send the mind spinning through space.

At five, however, my books went into the toy box and my mother enrolled me in more worthwhile activities—piano lessons, voice lessons, ballet lessons, personal training in poise and femininity. At six I entered my first beauty pageant.

Never mind that I was short and chunky, totally devoid of balance, and tone-deaf. I also had a penchant for wearing my brother's hand-me-downs and playing baseball in the vacant lot with the boys, and Mother was determined to nip those habits in the bud. She decked me in itchy pink dresses with multiple petticoats, patent leather shoes, and little socks with pink bows on the turned-down sides. I dutifully attended voice and piano and dance classes and even tried to learn to walk with a book on my head—Shakespeare, I think it was. Or George Eliot.

By the time I was ready for first grade, I knew better than to even suggest wearing white shoes after

Labor Day or before Easter. I knew how to use my limited feminine wiles to charm judges and make them forget that I couldn't sing my way out of a Piggly Wiggly sack. I knew how to curtsy and how to smile when I felt like spitting. I even knew how to flip my hair.

To all appearances, my mother's regimen for conforming her daughter to the expectations of a Southern Lady seemed to be working.

Until I went to school.

Once I entered the rank and file of the great untutored multitudes, my mother's Southern Lady refrain took on an altered tone. Now she had a different battle on her hands. Not only did she have to "bring me up right," she had to undo all the improper habits I was picking up outside the nest from my vulgar peers.

One of the worst idiosyncrasies I acquired in first grade was an unaccountable predilection for making friends with the wrong people. People like Dorrie Meacham, a sweet, sensitive, shy girl who wore braces on her legs from a bout with polio. . . .

Good grief. That was almost forty years ago. Until this minute I'd forgotten all about Dorrie Meacham. What else was I going to find buried back there in my brain, covered with four decades of dust and cobwebs?

Dorrie, an early reader like myself, wanted to see my collection of books, so one day she came home with me on the bus. Mama met us at the door with that fixed, frozen smile that always spelled trouble and watched like a hawk as Dorrie clanked awkwardly through the front parlor and down the hall to my bedroom. Mother gave us exactly eighteen minutes of blissful privacy before she came and stood in the doorway.

"Priscilla, haven't you forgotten something?"

I couldn't for the life of me think of what I had forgotten, but I scrambled to my feet and stood at attention, praying like thunder that some divine revelation would disclose my shortcoming before Mama had a chance to tell me. "Huh?"

"Ladies do not say 'huh,' Priscilla." She cleared her throat.

"Yes, ma'am."

"Now, wouldn't you like to introduce me to your little friend?"

My mind groped for the proper wording. "Mother, I would like you to meet my friend Dorrie Meacham. Dorrie, my mother."

"Nice to meet you, Mrs. Rondell," Dorrie said politely, struggling to her feet and offering a pale, thin hand.

"You seem like a very well-brought-up young lady, Dorrie."

My heart soared. Dorrie had passed the test. She had been polite, but not intrusive. Mother had declared her well brought up.

Or so I thought.

"Why don't you girls come into the kitchen for lemonade and cookies, and then I think it's time for Dorrie to go on home."

We sat at the table at right angles, uncomfortable, the spell of our budding friendship severed by my mother's palpable presence, the silence broken only by the tick-tick of the kitchen clock and the clunk-clunk of Dorrie's braces as they swung against the legs of her chair. When the glasses were empty, my mother, with that same icy smile on her face, ushered Dorrie to the door and thanked her for coming. I watched through the window as my friend—my only friend, if truth be told—limped down the sidewalk to the end of the block and disappeared behind the neighbor's house.

When I got back to the kitchen, Mother was on her knees beside the chair where Dorrie had sat, rubbing scratch cover into the wooden legs. She finished the task, put away the rag, and pointed to the chair. "Sit down, Priscilla."

I sat, dreading the tone in Mama's voice and the expectation of what was to come.

"What do you know about Dorrie Meacham, Priscilla?"

I squirmed. "Not much, I guess. She's in my class at school, and she likes to read, and she's real smart and funny—"

"Stop fidgeting, Priscilla. Ladies do not fidget."

"Yes, ma'am." I took a deep breath and clasped my hands on the table in what I hoped looked like a semblance of composure.

"And where does she live?"

"Three blocks over, on Duncan Street. Her father is—"

"Howard Meacham, the pharmacist. I know. And her mother is Elsie, who runs the cash register at the drugstore."

"Yes, ma'am."

Mama shook her head and narrowed her eyes. "Priscilla, I'm sure you feel sorry for Dorrie and were trying to help her. But you need to look for friends who are more—well, our kind of people."

I wasn't sure what that meant, didn't dare ask, and was pretty certain I didn't want to know anyway. To my six-year-old mind, Dorrie was my kind of people. She loved books, she was almost better at reading than I was, and she made me laugh. She was my first friend. My best friend.

"No doubt the Meachams are a very nice family, in their own way," my mother was saying. "But a Southern Lady can't be too careful who she socializes with. Your father and I have invited Dr. Thornton and his wife for dinner this Friday. Dr. Thornton is an important client of your father's. Their little girl Sarah is just about your age, and she's such a lovely child. Do try to get along with her, won't you, Priscilla? For my sake, if not for your own."

"Yes, ma'am." I gave the required response, but my heart wasn't in it. I knew Sarah Thornton, and she was just about the snobbiest, nastiest kid in school. She strutted around with her nose in the air, flouncing her blonde curls and looking down on everybody, including me. Just the day before, on the playground, she had bullied her way through a game of dodgeball, hitting Dorrie so hard she fell down and then making fun of her for not being fast enough to get out of the way. I wanted to snatch those curls right out of Sarah Thornton's scalp, to bloody that turned-up nose and teach her not to mess with my friend. But I didn't. I just helped Dorrie up and walked away with Sarah's high-pitched taunts ringing in my ears.

"Remember, Priscilla," my mother said as she got up from the table, "pity is no basis for friendship."

That night, as I lay in bed dreading Friday evening, when I would have to endure the company of Sarah Thornton and her parents—who were, according to Mama, "our kind of people"—I overheard a conversation between Mother and Daddy about Dorrie Meacham.

"The Meachams are working people with no name, no connections," Mama said, her voice rising. "I just don't think that's the kind of socializing we should encourage. In the long run, Priscilla will be so much better off if she learns early in life to choose more suitable companions."

Daddy's feeble protest reached me through the wall. "Donna, she's only a child. What difference does it make?"

"It makes a world of difference," Mother responded. "That little Dorrie is so pathetic. She obviously needs a friend, but—"

Mama lowered her voice and I couldn't hear any more. But I suspected that it wasn't only Dorrie Meacham's name and background that made the difference.

It was also because Dorrie was a cripple.

Dorrie never came to the house again, and even at school we gradually stopped talking and went our separate ways. That night I went to sleep crying because the first friend I had ever chosen for myself wasn't good enough.

It made me sick inside, sick with frustration and longing and confusion. It made me wonder if I could ever manage to be what Mama wanted me to be—a proper Southern Lady with proper values. After all, I had picked Dorrie as my friend. My mother had cast Sarah Thornton for the role.

But I was a Bell, of the Clarksville Bells, and the burden of responsibility fell upon me to make my mother proud. My mother, and all those generations of Bell women whose names were uttered at our christenings and cotillions. A Southern Lady could never just throw caution to the winds and follow her own heart. She did what was expected, at least if she was brought up right.

It was my first conscious glimpse of what being "brought up right" might do to my soul.

· 4 ·

The morning after my reluctant return to Chulahatchie, Mama went out to meet "the girls" for brunch at the country club. I was not invited.

Instead I took a Prozac, installed myself on the verandah with my journal, and reread what I had written the night before. I normally don't hear voices inside my head, at least not on a regular basis. But I couldn't silence my therapist's exhortation, echoing against the inside of my skull, nagging at me to continue exploring the nuances of my relationship with my mother.

Lovely.

I turned to a fresh page and wrote the first words that came to my mind:

Shit. Double shit. Holy shit.

Quite apart from the profanity issue, Mama would say that "holy shit" is an inaccurate metaphor, an oxymoron. A woefully imprecise analogy, like "cold as hell."

With all due respect, she's wrong. I've seen plenty of holy shit in my time. And a lot of holier-than-thou shit, too. Well-brought-up people dump it in your path every single day, like oblivious elephants lumbering along in the circus parade. And the rest of us spend our lives following behind with scoops and shovels.

What, I wondered, would the old fool make of *that* image?

My mother did her best, God knows. And I tried—I really tried—to be what she wanted me to be. But no matter how much effort I put into it, I seemed destined to be a lifelong source of disappointment to the woman who had given me birth and committed herself to bringing me up as a Southern Lady.

I stared at the words on the page and wondered if they were true. Had I tried hard enough? Could I have been what she wanted me to be if I had devoted more effort to it? And if I *had* turned out to be that perfect child, that Southern Lady, would I have been me at all, or would Peach Rondell simply have disappeared, like some defenseless earthling absorbed by an alien being with unlimited powers?

Over breakfast, Mama and I had spent a tense and uncomfortable hour looking at one of the numerous family scrapbooks she had so painstakingly created. She had chosen the one I despised most, the one where she could *ooh* and *aah* over what a beautiful little doll I had been as a child.

My customary response to this ritual was to sit in stony silence, while the soul within me battered at the bars of my cage like a trapped bird. All my life I have regarded Mama's photograph albums as a form of covert torture—hated the pictures, hated the cruise down memory lane, hated the implied disapproval of my present self in her effusive gushing over the past.

This morning, however, I had a different response. An unexpected epiphany.

Now I retrieved the album from the bookcase in the den and took it out to the wicker table on the porch. I positioned the album on my left and the journal on my right, opened both, and waited.

I'd looked at these photos a thousand times. But suddenly they appeared different, like a hidden code I could finally understand. Something secret, concealed in plain sight. You can pass by unseeing for years, and then once you see it, you see it. And once you see it, you can't imagine how you could have not seen it for so long.

Age Four: The Birthday Party. In a faded, brownish photo, a small girl stands at the head of a table full of prissy-looking children with their equally prissy-looking mothers arranged behind them. The candles on the cake are burning. Everyone is smiling—everyone except the birthday girl.

I'm surprised my mother kept this picture. It was probably my father who insisted upon including it in the photo album. He would have thought it funny. My mother, no doubt, was mortified.

In the picture, one side of my face is a distorted mass of purple bruises. One eye is swollen shut, and just at the moment the shutter clicked, I have lifted my dress up to my chin to scratch an itchy place on my stomach. My flowered panties are pushed down below my rounded tummy, showing my belly button.

I remember little of the occasion, and wouldn't recall the itch at all except that it is caught on film in all its candid honesty. What I do remember is what transpired three days before.

Mama, who was busy getting dinner, sent me and my brother, Harry, out to play on the porch. This was before we moved into Belladonna, and our "porch" was an enclosure that stretched across the back of the house and served as a combination pantry and playroom.

Mama's instructions were clear: Harry was to put his toy soldiers away in the trunk and I was to amuse myself with my play kitchen—a collection of miniature appliances crafted of heavy plywood by my grandpa

Chick. I had a little pink stove with an oven door that really opened, a pink cabinet with a tiny sink that pumped real water, and a toy refrigerator, also pink, which stood four feet high and was sturdy enough to stand on. It was every child's dream kitchen—every child who dreams about Pepto-Bismol, anyway.

No doubt my mother had put my grandfather up to this burst of creativity. The play kitchen had been my Christmas gift that year. I remember trying hard to look happy and not give in to tears when my brother unwrapped his present, also built by my grandfather— a bright red pickup truck, all wood, with a leather seat and pedals and a real steering wheel.

I didn't want my pink kitchen. I wanted Harry's red truck. But my mother clearly longed to see me playing house, so I pretended. I set up tea parties with the dolls I despised, and then when Mama wasn't looking, filched Harry's toy soldiers and drowned them in the sink. Once I even shoved a crab apple into my best doll's mouth and roasted her, stark naked, in the oven. Mama never understood why Harry called her Barbie-Q.

That afternoon, as Mother cooked dinner, I tried once more to enjoy playing with my kitchen. When I was bored nearly to tears, my brother came up with a brilliant idea.

"Come on, Peach, let's play Jack an' the Bean-stalk," he suggested, pointing to my pink refrigerator.

"I'll be Jack, you can be the giant, and we'll use your icebox for the beanstalk."

Sounded like a great idea to me—and a lot more interesting than a tea party or cooking a pretend meal for a pretend husband who would come in from the office, eat his pretend dinner, and then disappear to his den without even pretending to be grateful.

With some difficulty, I hoisted myself and my frilly little dress up onto the stove, and from there to the top of the play refrigerator. "Fee, fi, fo, fum!" I yelled in my best imitation of the giant's voice. "I smell the blood of an Englishman!" I knew the story, so I should have been prepared for what happened next.

Harry, playing Jack, began to chop down the beanstalk. He put all his heart and soul into the task, pushing against the plywood refrigerator until it began to rock precariously on the hard tiles of the porch floor. My patent Mary Janes, slick on the bottoms and with absolutely no traction, slid out from under me. Both the refrigerator and I came crashing down. I landed square on my head, and blood went everywhere. My brother stood over me hollering, "I win! I win!"

I don't recall much after that, except vague images of being snatched up and rushed to the hospital. A concussion, the doctor said—not life threatening, but I would have some pretty significant bruising. My father held an ice pack to my temple and murmured soothing words about how much he loved me and was glad I would be all right, and what a brave girl I was that I didn't cry. Even my sister, Melanie, who was seventeen and above us all, condescended to be nice to me.

My mother said, "Young ladies do not climb on kitchen appliances. It's just not done."

I hadn't planned it this way, not deliberately, but the outcome was more than I might have hoped for. The next day my father took my play kitchen to the garage and disassembled it. For years the neighbor's dog, a German shepherd named Bullet, suffered in embarrassed silence in a pink plywood doghouse.

I felt sorry for poor old Bullet. But getting rid of that pink kitchen was the best birthday present I ever received.

Age Five: The Christmas Pageant. In this picture, I am standing in front of the fireplace dressed in a flowing white gown, wearing iridescent wings trimmed in gold and a glittering halo. My hair—which is by nature straight as a Baptist preacher—is curled around my ears in a hideously fresh perm. I look like a Christmas ornament some demented child might make in Sunday school, using a Brillo pad for the head.

My expression in this snapshot is appropriately angelic. I am smiling graciously, looking off in the distance as if overcome by some heavenly vision. The truth was, I had a secret.

If you look closer, you'll see, beneath the floor-length hem of the angel's robe, a pair of black boots peeking out. Cowboy boots. Harry's boots. I couldn't have my own—it wouldn't be ladylike, you know—so I stole his.

I remember that Christmas pageant vividly—it was the most fun I ever had at a church function. I guarded my secret closely, and my mother never knew what I had done. Nor did my brother ever find his boots.

But to this day, my mother keeps a framed copy of that photograph on the big square grand piano in the front parlor. It reminds her, I suppose, of how proud she once was of her angel, her little lady.

Maybe someday I'll tell her. Meanwhile, every time I see it, it makes me smile.

Age Six: The Ballet Recital. Here we have a study in contrasts—Three Graces. Or, more aptly, Two Graces and a Dump Truck. The two lithe, slender girls showing off their poise for the camera are my cousins, Belinda and Cynthia. They're doing a perfect plié. I look like I'm squatting to pee.

I had seen my sister Melanie's ballet photographs. Hell, my parents even had a jerky black-and-white home video of her recital. I knew what I was supposed to look like—tall, willowy, graceful, smiling into the lights. Perfect.

Melanie was always perfect.

Clearly I was not Melanie, but my mother was a woman of great hope and purpose. What better way for a proper young Southern girl to learn grace and finesse than by taking dance lessons?

I'll give my mother credit—at least she attempted to make this torture bearable. On the principle, I suppose, that misery loves company, she enlisted my two cousins to join me. Twice a week, after school, we donned leotards and slippers and took our place at the bar. The dance instructor, a skeletal creature with protruding pelvic bones and veins in her neck the size of sixty-amp wiring, shouted to us over blaring classical music.

The teacher terrified me. She had long dark hair pulled back in a bun so tight it made her eyebrows arch into her hairline. I cannot recall her name, but once, in an art gallery, I saw her portrait—an expressionistic offering called *The Scream*. To this day I think of her as the epitome of a face-lift gone bad and wonder where Edvard Munch had the misfortune to meet her.

If, in my formative years, I suspected that I might not make it into the ranks of proper Southern Lady–hood, ballet class proved it beyond the shadow of a doubt. Belinda and Cynthia did their arabesques and chassés to perfection. My arabesque resembled the opening stance of a karate demonstration, and my chassé, as I see it in retrospect, looked like a hippo with hemorrhoids.

While the two of them won kudos from Madame de Sade and rapidly advanced to the head of the class, I struggled valiantly just to keep my leotard from crawling into my butt crack. "No, no, no!" she would shriek, her veins bulging and her eyebrows rising impossibly higher. "There is a name for this movement, this grabbing of the buttocks? No? Then it is not done in ballet. Eyes forward; one hand on the bar, the other extended—thus!"

The day Daddy shot the Three Graces photo was the worst day of all—our ballet recital, when the parents and friends of all these young lovelies gathered to sit in awed rapture as we danced for them. Belinda and Cynthia, of course, had prominent roles. Belinda was the lead swan; Cynthia, taller and even more graceful, with long blonde hair, had been cast as the princess.

They should have called it Swine Lake. When my turn came—I was the last swan, farthest from center stage, and nearly hidden by the backdrop—I waddled on for my three seconds in the limelight, a porker doing a pirouette, my sausage legs struggling furiously to keep up.

I made one leap successfully, albeit a mere two inches from the floor, but on the second, a glissade leading to a jeté, my balance failed me and I went tumbling tush over tutu. The audience laughed and applauded graciously, as if they knew I had meant to do it from the beginning.

Mother withdrew me from ballet class the following week. Cynthia and Belinda went to Ole Miss on performing arts scholarships. My mother's plans might have panned out, after all, if only she had been given the right sort of material to work with.

One lone photograph remains from my dance debut—this still life, showing two graceful swans and a stubby baby duckling. I like to think Mama kept it around to remind herself that you can't make a silk tutu out of a sow's behind, no matter how hard you work to bring the sow up right.

History, of course, assures me she had no such epiphany.

I shut the photograph album and put it away. ("A place for everything, and everything in its place," Mama always told me.) Then I sat for a while looking out into the yard at an angle, down toward the river bluff. It had rained in the night, and the sun had come out, dazzling the eye with diamond drops on every leaf and blade of grass. One of those glorious spring mornings you get in the South, when mist combines with sunlight to create magic and mystery.

My favorite book as a child was *The Secret Garden*, and the backyard at Belladonna had always put me in mind of the walled garden where miracles took place and mother-less children found healing and hope. My therapist would make a mountain out of that molehill, no doubt, finding all kinds of hidden significance in my identification with crippled, angst-ridden orphans. And perhaps he was right. Perhaps in my deepest subconscious I did feel abandoned and alone in the world. I certainly never fit in the world my mother had created.

The question that wouldn't let me go was, *Why did it matter so much?* I was forty-five years old, a grown woman, a fully developed and differentiated individual. And yet as soon as I set foot inside this house, some bizarre kind of mother-spell worked on me to turn me into a child again—*that* child, the one in angel wings and halo and stolen boots, the pudgy little porker in an ill-fitting tutu. The child who always tried so hard and always disappointed.

I asked Robert this very question once, back in the early days when we still tried to talk, when he still tried to care about what I felt and at least acted like he gave a damn if something hurt or upset me.

Against my better judgment, we had come to Chulahatchie for the holidays, one of Mama's huge elaborate Belladonna Christmases. "It's Christmas," he said. "What could possibly be so awful about being with your family for Christmas?"

He found out. The week had been tense and strained and full of false cheer, and the last night, lying in Robert's arms in my childhood bedroom, I cried and cried and asked him, "Why?"

"Because she's your mother," he said.

I twisted at the hairs that covered his chest. He hated for me to do this, but I couldn't seem to help myself; it was a comfort thing, like thumb sucking. He endured it for a while and then closed his hand over mine. "Mothers always hurt their daughters," he went on. "It's some kind of leftover evolutionary instinct, I think. Some fish eat their young, you know."

I didn't say anything. I sensed that he was winding up toward profundity, shifting into philosopher mode. I could almost feel the adrenaline pumping through his body as my hand lay on his chest, and I knew that once he got going, he was capable of holding forth half the night on almost any subject. Any residual concern for my feelings would soon dissipate in the energy of his thought processes.

God, the man did love the sound of his own voice.

"Perhaps," he said, "the navel itself is the primal wound inflicted by one's mother."

When Robert began to talk like this, he always adopted an intonation that signified a trumpet fanfare, a drumroll, a clash of cymbals. The ultimate *ta-da* that called everyone's attention to his intelligence.

"The umbilical cord is cut but never totally severed. We enter the world bleeding and crying and forever bear the scar that reaches inward, all the way to the core of our being."

Over the years I had come to despise Robert's philosophical turn of mind and the superior tone of voice that came with it, but I had to admit he had a point. A good one. Every woman I knew had issues with her mother. Every counselor I'd ever visited seemed to think that motherhood was the logical place to start in therapy. Even my current shrink, the old fool, recognized the grit of truth inside this pearl of a stereotype.

That's why he'd sent me home to Chulahatchie.

Disgusted with myself, I got up and tried to shake it off, this morose turn of mind. It was a beautiful day. I ought to get outside and soak up some vitamin D, quit moping around. And I ought to do it before Mama got back, or I'd be stuck for the day.

I dashed upstairs, retrieved my car keys, and bolted for freedom.

I was loitering in the produce aisle of the Piggly Wiggly, buying a cantaloupe to counteract the supreme deep-dish pizza and Bunny Tracks ice cream already in my cart, when I heard a voice behind me.

"You don't want that one."

I turned. "Excuse me?"

He smiled—a quirky, lopsided grin punctuated with a little apostrophe of a dimple at the corner of his mouth. "The cantaloupe. It's not ripe."

He came close enough for me to feel warmth emanating from him, catch a whiff of spicy cologne. I backed away, suddenly self-conscious and glad that, to pacify Mama, I had made the effort to put on makeup this morning.

"Let me show you." As he took the cantaloupe, his fingers brushed mine—deliberately, I thought, but that might have just been my imagination or wishful thinking. "You press here, on the navel, and if it's soft, the fruit is ripe."

"Since when do cantaloupes have navels?" I blurted out.

He laughed—a nice laugh, low and warm—then shrugged. "It's where the vine was connected, like the umbilical cord, so wouldn't that qualify as a navel?" He put the melon back on the pile, chose another one, and handed it to me. "Try this one."

"Okay, thanks."

He picked up an orange from the adjacent display, rolling it around in his hands like a baseball. "Do you think you might like to have coffee with me sometime?"

"Coffee? Sometime?" I repeated like a half-witted parrot.

He picked up two more oranges and started juggling them, right there in the produce section. "Sure," he said. "Coffee or tea, lunch or dinner, whatever." He kept his eyes on the flying oranges—up, over, around, faster and faster. "Say yes so I can stop."

I couldn't keep from laughing. "Okay, yes."

"Thank God." He caught the oranges, replaced them, and turned to face me. "I'm Charles," he said.

"I'm Peach." We looked at each other. I don't know what he saw, but I liked the view from where I stood. He was tall, with a boyish, round face, slightly receding hairline, and nice eyes. Not a hunk by any definition, not a movie star. Just a nice, ordinary, moderately attractive middle-aged man who looked into my eyes and seemed interested in getting to know me.

My eyes drifted to his left hand. No wedding ring, but—

He caught me looking and held it up for me to see. On the ring finger was the indentation, the echo of a band.

"Divorced," he said. "Or rather, in the process."

While he waited, I sidled back to the freezer section and replaced the Bunny Tracks and the deep-dish, double-cheese, super supreme pizza. No point in having spoiled Italian sausage, or getting melted chocolate and caramel all over my backseat, when I knew good and well I wasn't going home anytime soon.

I walked alone out to the parking lot of the Piggly Wiggly, got into my car, and followed his pickup to a truck stop out on the highway. He might have nice eyes and a funny little dimple and be able to juggle fruit, but I wasn't stupid enough to get into a truck with a man I'd just met. Even if I didn't think he was a serial killer, I've watched plenty of *CSI* in my time, and I wasn't taking any chances.

My single girlfriends had taught me the drill. Coffee first, in a public place.

Since it was so close to noon, it actually turned out to be lunch. Reuben on rye, with fries and a Diet Coke. We ate and made small talk and then settled down to the "get to know you" stuff over coffee and pie.

"Tell me about yourself," he said with forced casualness.

"There's not much to tell."

He smiled. "Don't be modest. I know Chulahatchie. You're the most interesting thing to come along in years."

It was a line, and I knew it, but I felt myself flush like a high school freshman anyway. This town was a small pond, and I had once been a pretty big fish. Was it possible he didn't know who I was?

Then the ludicrousness of the situation struck me. Except for the occasional duty visit and my father's funeral, I had been away for more than twenty years. I had left a beauty queen and returned a broken, middle-aged divorcée. I looked nothing remotely like Miss Ole Miss or second runner-up to Miss Mississippi.

Besides that, I didn't recognize him, either. Even if he'd been in Chulahatchie back in my glory days, he was older than I was, by ten years or more. When you're a teenager, you don't pay attention to people in their thirties and forties. They can live right next door, and if they don't appear in your orbit of reality, they don't exist.

Maybe he didn't know who I was or who I had once been. Maybe he did. It didn't much matter to me. What mattered was that he treated me as if I were the most fascinating and attractive creature he had ever met, and he gazed at me as if I were astonishingly beautiful.

If it was an act, it was a damn good one. Good enough to fool me. Good enough to make me not care if I was being fooled.

At least good enough for now.

In my own defense, my initial liaison with Charles Chase was a simple matter of heredity. It's all in my genes. That's g-e-n-e-s.

"You are a Bell," my mother has said to me on innumerable occasions throughout my childhood and adolescence—and well into my adulthood, if truth be told. "Remember your heritage; blood will tell."

As I wrote the words *blood will tell*, I felt an involuntary shudder course through me.

I first heard this phrase as a little girl, and it conjured up images in my mind that were light-years distant from what my mother intended. I was, as I have said, a voracious reader, and even as a child I knew from books that you could always track the murderer from blood samples at a crime scene.

That wasn't, of course, what Mama meant at all.

What she meant was that a girl's bloodline was her hidden source of strength and power, the trump card in the game of social acceptability. One's "people," the stock one came from, determined one's position on the social ladder. It was a Southern Lady's responsibility not only to know and revere her forebears, but to invoke the Hallowed Name to maintain or advance her position.

My grandmother GiGi, for example.

GiGi lived in rather modest surroundings, thanks to Grandpa Chick's drinking and gambling away the Barclay family fortune. But it never mattered that GiGi occupied a small white house filled with outdated furnishings. She was a lady. She was a Bell. She was the gravitational center of her own universe. And she never let anyone forget it.

Especially me.

Every summer we spent a couple of weeks at Grandma GiGi's house. I remember one of those long, steamy Southern afternoons in particular. I must have been five, or maybe almost six. It was before I went to school, at any rate. GiGi came and got me out of a nap, sat me down in the parlor, and, with wind from the electric fan ruffling the pages of history, took me on an extended tour through the Bell family album. Five generations of Bell women—six, if you included me. One hundred seventy years of Bellness.

Alberta Bell, my great-great-great-grandmother, was the matriarch of the Bell Plantation. In shadowy sepia images, she peered out from the family photographs as if examining me to see if I was worthy of the name.

"Alberta married well when she caught Adolphus Bell." My grandmother repeated this rhyming couplet like a mantra, like a magical incantation that would empower me to do the same. Dolph, as everyone called him, was the wealthiest boy in five counties, the only child of Langford

Bell, from the Chesapeake Bay area of Virginia. Alberta was—well, I never really found out who Alberta was or where she came from. Her history, as far as GiGi was concerned, seemed to begin with her marriage to Dolph. I suspect she might have been a poor girl from the wrong side of the tracks.

Poor, but smart. As young Dolph was preparing to come west, to use his daddy's money to make even more money growing cotton in Tennessee, Alberta convinced him that he should marry her by giving him to know that she was carrying his child.

A dozen other young lovelies around Chesapeake Bay might have made the same claim, my grandmother told me without a hint of disapproval, but Alberta made the most convincing case. She was not pregnant, of course— by Dolph or any other man, for that matter. But the ploy worked, and by the time he found out different, the hapless Dolph was hooked, reeled in, stuffed, and mounted over Alberta's fireplace.

What amazed me about Alberta's story was not that it involved sex, but that my own grandmother would tell me this tale with such obvious pride, as if Alberta had won the Nobel Prize for Manipulation by coercing Adolphus Bell into marriage under false pretenses.

GiGi made it clear, of course, that she didn't recommend this particular tactic, but in Alberta's case it worked, and apparently the end justifies the means if the outcome succeeds. Here she stood, straight and proud at the center of the Happy Family: Alberta and Dolph with their seven offspring, three boys and four girls. The boys, GiGi told me, bought land of their own adjacent to their father's and greatly expanded the holdings of the Bell Plantation. The girls married the eligible sons of their father's colleagues, and the extended family created sort of a feudal territory, a fiefdom ruled by the power of the Bell blood.

I wanted to ask my grandmother why the Bell name became the significant marker of our family's heritage rather than Alberta's maiden name, and whether or not there were other Bell descendants running around the Tennessee countryside—perhaps with darker hair and skin than the original blond, blue-eyed Bell clan. Given Adolphus Bell's obvious way with the ladies, I suspected there might be another side of my Bell heritage that nobody talked about.

But I didn't bring it up. That wasn't the point, anyway. The point was that Bell women, beginning with Alberta, married well, no matter how crooked the path that brought them to their nuptials. Alberta deserved Dolph. She got what she wanted, and then she brought her own daughters up to choose wisely, as she had. The Bell clan flourished, at least until the Yankees pillaged and plundered their way through the South. But even after the plantation house had been stripped to the bare walls and left like an empty skull amid the ruined cotton fields, the Bells still held on to their dignity, their place in society, and their name.

* * *

If blood will tell, it seems I got a disproportionate amount of Great-great-great-grandmother Alberta's DNA.

But I won't let Mama in on that little secret. I'll just let her think I took a long, long time picking out a cantaloupe at the Piggly Wiggly.

· 6 ·

I had promised my fool of a therapist that I'd call once a week and report on my progress. I told him about my journaling and the insights I was gaining about my family of origin, and I told him about my time with Mama and all the negative emotion that interaction called up in me. It was mostly psychiatric bull puckey, which he probably figured out in a nanosecond if he was even half awake, but it made us both feel better to go through the motions. Besides, he was getting eighty bucks an hour to pretend to listen, so I made sure he got my money's worth.

What I didn't tell him was that I was lying to my mother about going to the library when I was really meeting and mating Charles Chase at a secluded little fishing cabin on the banks of the Tennessee–Tombigbee Waterway.

* * *

The first time we went to the river camp, it was afternoon. Charles drove and I followed in my car without paying much attention, so I had a hard time finding the place by myself in the dark. In the end I had to call him on his cell phone three times and arrived frustrated and frazzled and feeling like a helpless airhead.

Charles didn't seem to notice. He met me at the car, took my hand, and escorted me up the steps to a porch that looked out over the river. I felt, however briefly, like Cinderella at the ball.

I had seen the cabin in daylight and knew it was rustic, but tonight it looked like a fairyland, with candles burning on every horizontal surface.

With his hand at the small of my back, he ushered me in, settled me on the sagging couch, and pressed a glass of white wine into my hand. "I made dinner," he said.

I concealed a smile and pretended not to notice the rotisserie chicken box from Piggly Wiggly on the kitchen counter.

He sat beside me with his arm thrown casually across the back of the couch, his thumb grazing my shoulder blade like an accidental touch. The contact galvanized all my senses from the neck down and left my brain groping in a fog.

We drank the wine, opened a second bottle, and took it out onto the screened porch where a single rose graced a table set for two. Night wrapped around us like a piece-work quilt, dark and warm and heavy. Beyond the screen I could see shards of moonlight floating on the surface of the water.

It should have been romantic. It was *planned* to be romantic, right down to the last detail.

Something was missing. But I'd had too much wine to be able to figure what it was or why making love with Charles Chase left me feeling sad and empty.

Maybe Great-great-great-grandmother Alberta's genes had not been diluted enough by the time they reached my twisted strands of DNA, but whether it was ancestry, destiny, or pure rebellion, I didn't much care.

He is irresistible. Or, to be more precise, the whole thing is irresistible. The sneaking around. The forbiddenness of it. The adrenaline rush. The giddiness. He makes me feel like a sexy, attractive, desirable woman, and I gravitate toward him like a hummingbird to sugar water.

Correction: He made me feel like a *girl*.

Just as I reverted to childhood the moment I started down the driveway toward Belladonna, now I rewound to a teenager at the merest thought of Charles Chase. Whenever he was close, all my nerves stood at attention, and when he wasn't around, I thought about him constantly.

Replayed conversations in my mind. Imagined his voice and his eyes and his smile. Wrote his name in the back of my journal, then tore the pages into confetti and threw them away. Daydreamed about him in the morning and fantasized about him at night.

It was idiotic. Even in the midst of it, I knew I wasn't in love. And when the emptiness and loneliness flooded over me in the backwash of our secret trysts, I had to push those feelings aside to keep from crying.

I had broken the first and only commandment of effective journaling: I wasn't telling the truth. I was writing what I *wanted* to feel, what I *wanted* to be true. Writing words that gave me an emotional fix in the moment, a fiction, a smoke screen, even as I knew that reality lurked just around the corner, waiting for me to acknowledge it.

But after Robert's rejection and the resulting meltdown of my self-esteem, lust seemed an acceptable substitute for love, and being the object of someone else's lust felt even better. Especially for a washed-out, aging beauty queen whose entire self-worth was built on the shifting sand of external appearance.

I had eyes; I could see what Robert saw, what Charles was seeing now. I wasn't blind to the crow's-feet and turkey wattle, the hip bulges and laugh lines. Maybe Charles was using me to bolster his own sagging ego, but if I was going to be absolutely candid, I was probably using him, too. The flat-out truth of it didn't make me feel particularly noble, but at least it was honest.

More honest than Great-great-great-grandmother Alberta.

More honest even than my own grandmother GiGi.

In June after my first year in school, Mama packed us up and took us to GiGi's house for the entire summer. We always went for a week or two, but this was different. There was a sense of urgency about it, a mission.

Everybody pretended this extended visit was designed to "give Mama a break," but I knew better. Ever since the ballet fiasco, it was crystal clear that Mama needed help if she intended to mold a recalcitrant child like me into the perfect little Southern Lady. There was only one viable alternative to utter despair: She called in reinforcements.

Her own mother, after all, had succeeded with her. And two heads were better than one.

My brother, Harry, came, too, but only by default. Melanie was nineteen and spending the summer at the lake with some college friends. Daddy had his law practice to tend to, and Harry, who was only nine although he seemed to think he was eighteen, couldn't very well stay at home alone during the day.

Harry, being a boy and therefore not a suitable candidate for my mother's training program, was pretty much left to his own devices. My grandparents lived in Waterford, a small, clean, segregated town in northern Mississippi. Waterford boasted a brand-new swimming pool, a fishing dock on the river, and a town square with a movie theater and an ice cream parlor, so Harry might as well have died and gone straight to heaven. For two months he lived out his dream of masculine freedom, walking wherever his fancy took him and gloating over the independence granted to him solely on the basis of his genitals.

The cynic in me thinks some things never change.

All that summer Harry made new friends on the baseball diamond and at the pool, went fishing with them, watched movies like *Butch Cassidy* and *The Love Bug* and slurped down milk shakes with abandon. I, on the other hand, lived as a prisoner, trapped in a never-ending circle of social correction with Mama on one side and my grandmother on the other.

I was nearing my seventh birthday—too young, most people would think, to be subjected to such rigors, too immature to understand the principles imposed upon me. But people often underestimate a child's ability to comprehend. Besides, my mother lived by the philosophy that it was never too soon to shape my sensitive soul into the model of Southern Lady–hood. The fresher the clay, the easier the molding.

Although I did not, at that young age, have the vocabulary to articulate all I learned that summer, my eager, questioning mind absorbed everything—a lot more, if truth be told, than my mother and grandmother could have known. In later years, when my analytical self began to sift through the accumulated layers of childhood experience, truths came to light that were far different from what my maternal forebears intended to teach me.

The memories overtook me. They poured out like reservoir water through a broken dam, drowning me, leaving me exhausted and gasping for breath.

It was a turning point. That summer of my sixth year changed forever the way I saw my mother, my grandmother, and myself.

My grandmother, Georgia Bell Posner Barclay—called GiGi by her grandchildren—was my mother's polar opposite. GiGi was as submissive as Mama was dominant. As a child I adored GiGi and my grandfather, called Chick, precisely because they were unlike the parents I lived with on a daily basis. But that summer I began to understand that, where Mother controlled overtly, by exerting her will, GiGi controlled covertly, through sheer sweet passivity.

I wasn't the only one who loved GiGi. The whole town of Waterford adored her, worshipped at her shrine, held her up as the example of the perfect Southern Lady. Georgia Bell Posner Barclay wasn't a woman, she was an institution.

GiGi and Chick didn't have money to speak of—not by that time, anyway. In years past, according to family legend, Grandpa Chick had a fortune laid at his feet. His father, whom everyone including Chick called Uncle Bark, had somehow managed to survive the Depression with his lumber business intact. He had pulled strings with some senator and landed a contract to provide materials to the WPA for work projects, so when the Depression lifted, he still had his silk shirts and a tidy little bank account, to boot. And he only had one child—Clayton Barclay, my grandfather. When Uncle Bark keeled over at age fifty-two from a heart attack, Chick inherited everything—a financial legacy that should have kept him and my grandmother in style for the rest of their lives.

But Chick had unique gifts. If my grandmother GiGi was known in Waterford as the saint, Chick was the sinner. In less than a decade he had managed to fritter away his fortune through stupid investments, general irresponsibility, and more than a few trips to the greyhound track in West Memphis.

By the time Harry and I came along, GiGi and Chick lived in a modest little white house on the corner of Third and Elm. Chick always made a show of being the man of the house—the ruler of the castle and the protector of the Little Woman. But now he worked as a distribution clerk in the lumber mill that still bore his family's name, and he hadn't owned a silk shirt in twenty-five years.

Grandpa Chick cut a compelling figure, with his broad shoulders and his fine head of thick white hair. He always had ruddy cheeks and a booming laugh, and he would take me on his lap and tickle me until I cried and begged for mercy. But I had seen him, too, when he smelled of whiskey and walked with a crooked gait. I had lain awake in the attic bedroom and listened, breathless, as his slurred voice grew louder, yelling at GiGi; as much as I loved him, I was a little afraid of him, too.

Everybody in Waterford knew what GiGi had given up for Chick. She could have been a woman of substance, they said, with a fine house and an inheritance to pass on to her children. She could have divorced him and married someone who was worthy of her. God knows she had enough reason, with his drinking and gambling and carousing.

But instead she had stayed, being true to the vows she had solemnly taken thirty years before. She had accepted her lot in life and, for better or for worse, devoted herself to making something of Chick. Saint Georgia had martyred herself upon the altar of matrimonial fidelity, giving up her own life for her husband's.

Sweet GiGi. Loving GiGi. Faithful, dedicated, blessed GiGi, doing her best to hold her reprobate husband to the straight and narrow. I, too, thought she was a genius and a candidate for canonization—until I got a glimpse of how she did it.

Cooter Randolph, the local bootlegger, was well known for supplying moonshine to most of the male population of Waterford and three surrounding counties. My grandfather was no exception, and GiGi had made up her mind to put a stop to it once and for all.

One hot summer afternoon I followed her, keeping out of sight as she picked her way through the woods to Cooter's place. She wore a pale lavender shirtwaist and stockings, white gloves, and a little hat with purple pansies on one side. When she got to Cooter's still, she found herself looking down the double barrel of a squirrel gun, and I had visions of throwing myself in the line of fire to save her life.

But GiGi didn't blink an eye. She simply settled herself carefully on a rotting stump, adjusted her gloves, and said softly, "Cooter, we need to have ourselves a little chat."

I'd heard about Cooter, but I'd never seen him before. Word had it that he'd spent time in the state penitentiary for killing a man who stumbled onto his land by accident. Shot him dead, square in the chest, people said, without asking a single question. Another time, he supposedly cut a man's hand off with an ax for trying to steal a jar of hooch without paying for it.

Cooter Randolph, rumor asserted, wasn't somebody you'd want to mess with. But up close, he didn't look like a murderer or a monster. He was just a broken-down, sad old man, riddled with palsy and poisoned by alcohol. He was tall and lanky, with four days' growth of beard and a mouthful of rotten yellow teeth. His eyes, bleary and bloodshot, swept over my grandmother with a pathetic, pleading expression. He cleared his throat and squirted a stream of tobacco juice through the space between his front teeth, then shakily lowered himself to a stump facing hers.

"Reckon I been expecting you, Miss Georgia," he said.

Behind him I saw the tools of his trade: the rusty still with its coils of copper wire, the slow-burning fire under the distilling pot, the lines of clay jugs and mason jars waiting to hold the home brew as it dripped out the end of a slender pipe. The air in the clearing held mingled scents of wood smoke and corn liquor.

GiGi stared him down. "If I'm not mistaken, Cooter, you've been selling moonshine to Clayton again, haven't you?"

He hung his head like a schoolboy reprimanded for rowdiness in the classroom. "Yes'm."

"I thought we had an understanding about this."

"Yes'm. But—"

"But what, Cooter?" Her voice was gentle and entreating.

"But I gotta make a living, Miss Georgia. Times is hard, and—"

She reached out and patted his grimy arm. "I know, Cooter. I understand. And I sympathize, you know I do. But you also know how I feel about moonshine whiskey. Especially when it finds its way into my husband's hands."

He began to shake all over. "You're not gonna sic the sheriff on me, are you, Miss Georgia? Doc says I got me a bad liver, and if I had to go to jail, well, I wouldn't make it, I swear to God I wouldn't."

She paused and thought for a minute. "You're not a married man, are you, Cooter?"

He grunted. "Was, once."

"And you live in the cabin back there?" GiGi pointed with an immaculate, white-gloved finger toward a shack that had nearly given itself back to the woods.

He nodded. His gaze bumped hers and then careened away.

"All right," she soothed. "Here's what we'll do. You stop selling your home brew to my husband, and I'll see to it that you get a hot meal every day. You look like you could use a good meal, couldn't you, Cooter?"

He grinned sheepishly and nodded. "Yes'm. Ain't et much of late."

"I'll make the arrangements. We have an agreement?" She gave him an odd, cold smile.

"Yes, ma'am, I reckon."

"I'm glad we understand one another." GiGi got up and straightened her skirt. "I'll be on my way, then."

Cooter jumped to his feet. "Sorry for troubling you, Miss Georgia. It won't happen again."

"I'm sure it won't, Cooter," she said smoothly. "Very sure."

He gave her a gentlemanly nod, just short of a bow. "I'd take you back to the road, Miss Georgia, 'cept I gotta guard my still."

"I can show myself out." She said it as if she were making her exit from a summer cotillion. And then my grandmother turned her back on Cooter Randolph and his still and his loaded shotgun and went home the way she came.

All the way back to town, I shadowed my grandmother and watched her walking, head held high, the little pansies on her hat bobbing gently. She was a true lady, I thought, showing care and concern for those less fortunate. She had treated even the likes of Cooter Randolph with respect. She was going to provide meals for him so that he wouldn't starve to death out there in the woods. A true humanitarian, my grandmother— seeing to the needs of a poor alcoholic bootlegger. I felt both proud and humbled to bear the Bell and Posner names.

Later that evening my insulating bubble of familial euphoria burst. I was sitting on the back stoop eating a slice of watermelon, which GiGi would not allow in the house, and overheard her and my mother talking about the encounter with Cooter Randolph.

"You told him you would provide hot meals for him?" My mother's low laugh held a note of mocking reprimand. "I don't believe it, Mother. You lied!"

"A lady never lies," GiGi corrected haughtily. "I told him I would see to it that he got a hot meal every day. And that's exactly what I did. He'll be well fed in jail."

Jail? My grandmother, the sweet saint of Waterford, was sending that poor sick old man to jail?

"Clayton led me right to Cooter's place," GiGi went on, "and never even knew I was following him. Sheriff Ketchum has been looking for that still for months. Now he's got himself an anonymous tip, directions good as a road map, straight out there. By this time tomorrow that engine of evil will be smashed into a thousand pieces and burned, and if that old shack goes up in the blaze as well, so much the better. No one will ever know I had a thing to do with it."

Passive. I had always thought my grandmother to be the passive kind of Southern Lady. It had never entered my mind that a passive lady could get her own way and still find a way to maintain her unsullied reputation for sweetness. In later years, when I took psychology and first encountered the term *passive-aggressive*, I had an image in my mind, just waiting for a label: GiGi, facing down Cooter Randolph's shotgun, her spine ramrod straight and her eyes filled with a cold, calculating smile.

I couldn't finish my watermelon. My throat was tight and my eyes swam with tears, and a wavery vision of Cooter's sad, broken countenance rose up in my mind. Jail would kill him, I was certain, and if it didn't, what did he have to come back to? The charred remains of a cabin he once called home? The memory of being deceived, his pathetic life snatched out from under him by a graciously conniving Southern Lady?

In that moment, my adulation of my grandmother was crushed beyond repair. Her sainthood. Her honeyed passivity. It had all been an act. A damn good act, but an act nevertheless.

Cooter Randolph never sold another drop of hooch to Grandpa Chick—or anyone else, for that matter. He died six weeks into his three-month sentence and was buried without ceremony in the no-man's-land between the white folks' graveyard and the plots reserved for the Negroes. From that day forward, the boss at Barclay Lumber hand-delivered my grandfather's paycheck to GiGi every Friday. And the banker, Mr. Longchamps, wouldn't give Chick a dime out of his own account without first making a telephone call to Miss Georgia for approval.

The woods, after all, were full of Cooters, and Chick would find them if he had a dollar in his pocket. She did it all, I heard GiGi tell Mama, for Grandpa Chick's own good.

I fleshed out the story in as much detail as I could remember, then I sat for a long time thinking about my great-great-great-grandmother's manipulation, my grandmother's deception, my mother's control. At last I began to write again:

Is this the legacy of the Bell women, the heritage I am destined to perpetuate?

Some women, like my mother, dominated by exerting the considerable force of their will. Others, like GiGi, did it through manipulation, while maintaining the facade of sweet femininity and submissiveness. But the effect was the same: A Southern Lady always got what she wanted. And if she was really good at it, as my grandmother was, she came out looking like the long-suffering victim of other people's insensitivity. A model of righteous forbearance. A martyr.

The day Cooter Randolph went to jail, the fragile web of my childish innocence began to unravel. Saint Georgia's halo began to tarnish. And I, at the tender age of not-quite-seven, first set foot on a path that would prove to be the undoing of my mother's plans to make me into a Southern Lady.

In that initial moment of sympathy for poor sick Cooter Randolph, I did something unimaginable, unthinkable.

I took up for the underdog.

7

Once Harry was settled into his daily routine of fishing, baseball, movies, and milk shakes, Mama and GiGi got down to the business of my "training."

It was sheer torture, and the oddest thing about it was that the two of them seemed to think that I should enjoy it, that I should be having fun. Or if I wasn't enjoying it, I should at least act as if I was. It was a lesson I was slow to learn, this art of pretense.

One of the prime directives that governs the actions of a Southern Lady is that she never, under any circumstances, allows others to feel uncomfortable in her presence. In her role as hostess, she serves as catalyst between her guests, smoothing over any ruffled feathers, smiling, calming the waters.

For six and a half years of my young life, I had seen that false expression on my own mother's face, but I did not as yet have powers of articulation sufficient to explain it. The forced, fixed smile that did not reach her eyes, the mask of congeniality. She had worn it the day she ushered my friend Dorrie to the front door and out of my life forever, and she wore it any time other people—particularly people who irritated her—were in her presence. A Southern Lady, after all, did not give in to negative emotions. Appearances had to be maintained at all cost.

This genteel affability, however, did not seem to apply with members of one's own family. It was connected, in some mystical, metaphysical way, with the hinges on the front door. When the door was shut behind the final guest, the mask vanished and the real feelings reasserted themselves. To my six-year-old mind this translated into: You have to be nice to people you don't like, but you can be as nasty as you want to people you love.

The whole principle of mannerly pretense confused and frustrated me, especially because my mother was completely intractable on the issue of lying. She didn't use the word "lie," of course. She called it "prevarication." No doubt I was the only first-grader in the nation who could spell, define, conjugate, and use the verb "to prevaricate" without a second thought.

And, much to my mother's dismay, I had a tendency toward prevarication. I came by it honestly enough: My father, as I have said, was an accomplished story-teller, and he rarely let a conscience scrupulous about truth get in the way of a good tale. If it told well, with sufficient drama or pathos or humor, he would tell it. And then retell it, with appropriate elaborations and editorial changes, depending upon his audience.

Mama, however, had no patience for telling stories. And when I told one—when I prevaricated, or even stretched the truth a little, just for effect—she would give me a lecture that made my little ears burn.

My mother never spanked me. Her lectures—or even her silent, reproachful glances—were enough to cow me into submission. When she cleared her throat, I would drop whatever I was doing and stand rigid, wait-ing to be corrected. Once, when I was about five, I was sprawled on the parlor rug, engrossed in a book, when she walked into the room and coughed. Twice.

I jumped up, my heart pumping, my mind scram-bling to know what I had done wrong so I could con-fess it—with tears, if necessary. She stared hard at me, standing there at attention, waiting for my punish-ment, and for just an instant her expression softened into something like sympathy.

In that fleeting moment, I thought she was going to apologize, to say, "I'm sorry I've been so hard on you."

Then she put a hand to her throat. "I think I'm coming down with a cold," she said and went into the bathroom to rummage in the medicine cabinet for the cough syrup. We never spoke of the incident, but for years I lived on the hope of seeing that soft spot reappear.

Nothing got my mother's ire up like falsehood, but she seemed not to see the connection between lying and the kind of social charade she and my grandmother tried to instill in me during that long hot Mississippi summer.

"A Southern Lady is always polite and gracious, Priscilla, no matter what she thinks of a person." GiGi repeated the words for what seemed like the hundredth time. "She smiles and engages in small talk and always looks interested in what others are saying."

I had seen the technique close-up, in my grandmother's interaction with Cooter Randolph. And although I had admired her act at the time, the ultimate outcome of the charade gave me a funny feeling in my stomach.

On the surface it was a nice, thoroughly Southern idea—being polite to people even if you couldn't stand their guts. But beneath that upper crust ran an underground stream of poisoned water, and I had witnessed for myself what kind of damage it could do when unleashed. It reminded me of "Little Red Riding Hood," the wolf disguised in Grandma's nightclothes. What big teeth it had, this custom of cordial duplicity.

I had plenty of opportunities that summer to practice smiling and small talk. Every day, it seemed, either we had ladies in for tea or we went to their homes. Most of them were my grandmother's friends, some of them teetering on the verge of senility, but all of them proper ladies. Right down to crazy old Letitia Sutterfield, who kept insisting that her grandson's Yankee fiancée was a Soviet spy who had been sent to snuff her out and steal her inheritance to further the cause of Communism in the Free World.

"I know, Tisha." My grandmother patted the old woman's hand and offered her a tea cake. "Just like Mata Hari. But don't you worry, everything will be all right." She said the proper words, but when Miss Letitia wasn't watching, she sent a glance to my mother that spoke volumes. The old biddy ought to be locked up, the expression said. For her own good, of course.

I sat clutching my teacup, vacillating between two contradictory sets of emotions. On the one hand, I was tempted to join in the laughter at the old loony's expense. But on the other, I felt sorry for her. She might be a little daft, but she was a dear old soul who truly— if misguidedly—believed her fears to be grounded.

My upbringing wouldn't permit me to contradict my mother and grandmother to their faces, and my conscience wouldn't let me make poor old Letitia Sutterfield the butt of a cruel joke. I sat there like a stone, my jaws frozen in a Southern Lady smile. It was, in my mother's favorite expression, a "learning experience."

Before the summer was over, I had the vacant smile down pat. Small talk was more difficult to master.

Apparently one of the hallmarks of a true Southern Lady is the ability to carry on extended conversation without expressing an opinion or offending anyone. Innocuous phrases such as, "Oh, really?" and "Isn't that interesting?" and "Well, imagine that!" littered the tearoom like so many discarded napkins. I never heard a single word I thought interesting—except perhaps Miss Letitia's story about the spy. Most of the conversation seemed designed to atrophy the imagination rather than stimulate it. But I watched in fascination and wonder as my mother and grandmother played the game, always with that smile on their faces, until the door closed with a groaning finality and the afternoon tea had come to an end.

There was one person that summer whom I found genuinely interesting: my grandmother's "girl," Molly-Faith Johnston.

Molly, who couldn't have been a day under sixty, was a large, buxom black woman with kinky white hair and shiny skin. Molly and her husband, Stick, worked for GiGi and Grandpa Chick. Stick kept the yard and did odd jobs, and Molly came at nine A.M. every weekday morning to do the laundry, cleaning, and cooking.

GiGi insisted that Molly and Stick were "part of the family," but even at age six, I knew better. Family didn't sit on the back stoop with plates in their laps to have their dinner while everybody else sat in the dining room around the big table.

I adored Molly, and I was fascinated by her. She had a big hearty laugh and a soft cushiony hug, and she didn't talk down to me or act as if my questions were stupid or unimportant. She sang Negro spirituals in a low, melodious voice as she worked, and when I asked her what they meant, she told me about her ancestors who came to Mississippi in the dark hold of a slaver's ship to work the plantations. She talked about freedom and hope and her precious Jesus, who loved all people no matter what the color of their skin.

"Lawd, child," she said one day when I had been sitting on a stool at her elbow for an hour, "ain't nobody never told you about your heritage? Look at them brown eyes. You sho 'nuff got somebody in the woodpile somewhere!"

She laughed until tears ran down her broad black nose, and then she went on to tell me about how white masters in the South had often fathered mulatto children out of the pretty young girls who worked in their houses and tended their fields. This was news to me, news that fascinated and alarmed me. I knew enough about men and women to know that this was possible, but I had never considered the ramifications. I had always been taught that the races never mixed. According to my mother and grandmother, my Bell heritage was lily-white and unsullied.

Now Molly was laughing, pointing to my brown eyes as evidence that some of the Bells—including me, apparently—might well have a drop or two of African blood in their veins.

The idea didn't offend me in the least—on the contrary, it intrigued me. It gave me a reason for the sense of connection I had with Molly, and it left me with a feeling of power. It was deliciously dangerous, this possibility that I, as a Bell-Posner and a budding Southern Lady, might be carrying some clandestine genetic aberration that my family had kept hidden from the world.

I had been taught about the War Between the States, of course, how my ancestors had fought bravely, if vainly, to hold on to their plantations and their lives. I had been told how the Bells treated their "nigras" well, how they loved them and cared for them as one might care for a beloved family pet. But I never, until that moment, considered the other side of the story.

It was the second step on my downward slide, the second opportunity I had that summer to identify with the untouchables. I didn't tell my grandmother or my mother, of course—I had learned my lesson from the incident with Cooter Randolph, and I had no intention of seeing Molly become the next victim of my grandmother's machinations.

I kept my thoughts to myself, cherishing them, hiding them away, pondering them in my heart. My conversations with Molly aroused a feeling in me that took years for me to identify and understand. All I knew at the time was that it was a good feeling, a feeling of being privy to some great secret of life that my family did not know—or if they knew, refused to acknowledge.

All that summer I divided my time between the training sessions Mama and GiGi devised for me and those treasured hours in the kitchen, soaking up Molly's wisdom and hope and love. And the more time I spent with Molly, the more hollow and false seemed the social graces that were being drilled into my childlike head.

Mother thought the summer was a great victory, a brilliant idea, a smashing success. I had learned to set a beautiful table and to carry myself with some semblance of grace—or if not with grace, at least with less awkwardness. I had mastered the art of smiling, holding a teacup without rattling it, and looking interested during inane conversation. I had been taught to think before speaking, to be polite to obnoxious people, to keep my voice down.

What Mama didn't know was that I had learned another lesson, one she never considered teaching me. It was Molly-Faith Johnston's lesson, taught more by example than by precept: to cherish my private opinions and not let anyone convince me against the witness of my own heart.

To be true to myself.

8

I'm writing it all in my journal. All the memories, all the
details of those early days with Mama and GiGi as they
tried to conform me to the image of the perfect Southern Lady and prepare me for my debut into the world of
beauty pageants. All the feelings, the contradictions. Pages
and pages of it. Raw, unedited footage of my upbringing,
my reluctant transformation from the angel in stolen boots
to the Bean Queen and Miss Ole Miss.

Loath as I am to admit it, maybe my therapist was right.
Coming home to these familiar haunts of my childhood—
to Mama, to Belladonna, to Chulahatchie itself—calls
up all manner of things I thought I'd forgotten forever.
God knows they're not necessarily happy memories, but a

girl's got to have something to show for being a psychiatric stereotype.

I'd love to believe that personal insight comes naturally, inevitably, like hemorrhoids, gray hair, and liver spots. It would make this whole process a heck of a lot easier. I wouldn't have to work so hard; all I'd have to do is wait. But then I look at Mama and realize that if wisdom automatically comes with age, she must've found the Fountain of Immaturity somewhere around age six, because she has yet to get past the notion that the world revolves around her.

As my shrink constantly reminds me, I cannot control the choices other people make. I can only choose how I respond. I'm trying to learn how to be a thermostat rather than a thermometer, but even when you carry your own weather with you, mothers have a way of changing the forecast and stirring up storms without warning.

Like today.

"Priscilla," Mama said, "I wish to speak with you."

I pried my eyelids open, groped for my watch on the bedside table, and squinted at the dial. Six forty-five. In the *morning*.

For the entire duration of my eighteen-year incarceration under Mama's roof, I never needed an alarm clock. Every blessed morning of my life, she came to the door of my bedroom and woke me—usually with some criticism primed and ready, as if it were a mortal sin to waste a single moment of daylight in the quest to correct my errant ways.

"God help me," I groaned. "Can't you give me a break? I got in late last night."

"Precisely," she said. "Breakfast will be served on the verandah in fifteen minutes."

Coffee. If she wasn't going to let me sleep, I needed coffee. Maybe laced with a little hair of the dog. I got up and dragged myself downstairs, barefoot, still in my striped seersucker pj's.

I knew she'd have something to say about the pajamas. Mama hates them—not just this pair, but any pajamas. She insists that no self-respecting lady would wear them and points to her own collection of satin gowns and matching peignoirs as an example of appropriate nightwear. She even has coordinating slippers with little furry pom-poms.

I suspect she's channeling the ghost of Loretta Young, but I wouldn't dare say so out loud.

The fragrances of coffee and bacon lured me toward the back of the house, and I detoured into the kitchen, where Mama's "girl," Matilda, was standing at the stove. We called her Tildy. She was sixty-three, nearly six feet tall and skinny as a pole bean, with kinky gray hair and rich brown skin and enormous flat feet. When she caught sight of me, she pulled the frying pan off the fire, set it aside, and wiped her hands on her apron.

"Hey, baby girl." Tildy opened her arms and hauled me

into a bony hug, pressing my whole head flat against her chest. I could hear her heart thunking against her rib cage, as clearly as if I were listening with a stethoscope. Strong and steady and reliable, like Matilda herself.

She smelled like bacon and magnolias. I made a mental note of the interesting juxtaposition so I could detail it in my journal later. It might have just been lemon dishwashing detergent, but I liked the idea of magnolias so much better.

"How's my sweet Peach?" she said. "And how come we ain't had time to talk since you got home?"

"You know how I'm doing. Mama tells you everything."

Tildy grinned. "Reckon she does. I's sorry to hear 'bout you and Robert."

I felt tears sting my eyes, and I blinked them away. "I'm okay."

"You're not," she said. "But you will be. You got grit."

"I've got grits?" I laughed. "Well, I certainly hope so. If they're your grits, that is."

Tildy shook her head. "With jalapeño cheese, just like you like 'em. I'm guessing you want your eggs scrambled soft with green onion. Fresh biscuits in the oven."

"Perfect," I said. "We'll talk later. I've gotta get some coffee and go face the dragon."

"Your mama got her hackles up about something?"

I shrugged. "Is she still breathing?"

Tildy giggled like a schoolgirl and ducked her head. "You bad, girl. You *real* bad."

"Maybe. But I notice you're not contradicting me."

Tildy shooed me out of the kitchen and off toward the back verandah, where Mama was waiting.

Belladonna faces east toward the morning light, so even in the heat of summer, the back verandah stays shaded and cool until midafternoon. Mama sat at the white wicker table in full makeup, wearing a flowing lavender gown, robe, and matching slippers, and looking as if she really believed herself to be a movie star subject to being photographed at a moment's notice.

At this hour of the morning, the bricks were downright chilly against my bare feet. I poured a steaming mug of coffee from the pot on the sideboard, sat down, and tucked my feet under my butt. One glimpse at Mama's face, and I wished I could hide my soul as effectively.

The woman had never had a private thought in her life, at least where her family was concerned. In public, she could maintain a gracious facade with the best of them and keep up a ladylike pretense whether she was bored to distraction or seething mad.

But with us, even when she kept her mouth shut, which didn't happen often, her face blabbed every single thing that was on her mind. This morning she had that pinched, raisin-faced look of disapproval. I swear, if she could see herself in the mirror and realize what kind of wrinkles that expression brought out, she'd never recover.

I sipped my coffee and waited. She waited. The tension between us stretched out thin as spun sugar, and when it was just about to snap, we both spoke:

"Priscilla, you're an adult and it's none of my business, but—"

"Look, Mama, I'm an adult and this is none of your business—"

If it had been anyone but my mother, we would have cracked up laughing. At least we agreed on two things: that I was an adult and that my life was none of her business.

Except for that one innocuous little syllable: *but*.

"But" was the qualifier that ruled my mother's life and spoiled every encouraging word that might have come out of her mouth.

You look very pretty, dear, but . . .

Of course I like your new boyfriend, but . . .

Certainly I want you to be happy, but . . .

Nothing was ever good enough. In the fourth grade, I landed the role of Glinda the Good Witch in our elementary school production of *The Wizard of Oz*, beating out a half dozen sixth-graders, but she was convinced I should have been Dorothy. When I weighed 122, she thought I could stand to lose another five pounds. After I won the title of Mississippi Soybean Queen at the state fair, she started planning for the Miss Ole Miss Pageant before the shine was off the tiara. And never mind her response when I only got second runner-up to Miss Mississippi.

Despite a lifetime of examples to the contrary, I naively believed that getting engaged to Robert, a rising star among the young professors at UNCA, might be sufficient. But no. She thought I might have done better marrying a *real* doctor rather than a mere Ph.D. "After all," she said, "he's not the kind of doctor who can actually *help* anybody."

So here came Mama again, showing her buts: "It's none of my business, but . . ."

I sighed and took a long swig of coffee. "But what?"

"I know you've been seeing someone; don't deny it. And yes, you're a grown woman who can make her own decisions, but isn't it a little early to get involved in another relationship? You're still a married woman."

"Technically," I said, "I'm a legally separated woman. For six months now."

"Five," she corrected. "But that's not the point."

"All right, five and a half," I said. "So what is the point?"

"The point is, Chulahatchie's a small town. Everybody knows everybody. Everybody knows everybody's *business.*"

"The point is," I said, "you're worried about what people will think of *you.*"

"Of course I am," she said without hesitation. "I am

your mother. Now, just who is this person? Is he our kind of people? Are you being discreet?"

The woman was certifiable. She didn't care whether I was having an extramarital affair. She only cared whether he was someone with a good name and a good family lineage.

The right kind of adulterer, the kind who would make a mother proud.

The right kind of people. Our kind of people.

Not as easy a distinction as one might think.

Many non-Southerners mistakenly believe that Southern society is divided into two categories: white and black. Certainly my family believed in and upheld the principle of separation of the races—as my mother was fond of saying, feathers and fins belong to two different species. (The mammal misconception is a common defense for racism in the South.)

To my credit—although the temptation was great, especially during my teenage years—I did manage to avoid bringing up the reality of seagoing mammals and furry land creatures who deliver their offspring through the laying of eggs.

Besides, racism was not really the central issue. When the civil rights movement began to exert its inexorable influence in every area of Southern life, I found—much to my surprise—that my mother could accept a black family in the church as long as they were beautiful and educated and articulate and resembled the Obamas. As long as the husband was a doctor or a lawyer and wore nicely tailored suits; as long as the wife was slim, light skinned, and fashionable; as long as the children (no more than two of them) were well behaved and didn't wear braids sticking out all over their heads. And, of course, as long as said children did not wish to date or marry the little white children.

Prejudice by classism. The conviction that intelligent, thoughtful, professional, white-collar Christians should pretty much keep to their own.

This was no doubt easier before the onset of egalitarian twentieth-century culture, where it's not always a simple matter to determine who are and who are not "the right kind of people." Black people were generally not the "right kind," although they did have their accepted place in society as long as they knew how to stay there.

White people were a little more difficult to differentiate, particularly for a child—even a child as bright as I was. The state did, after all, let just anyone attend the public schools, no matter what their name or heritage. It was often a matter of trial and error to discover which friends would be acceptable in my mother's eyes.

I had learned the hard way that following my instincts made me vulnerable to unreliable information.

My little friend Dorrie seemed to have all the qualifications: She was kind, polite, well brought up, intelligent, and dressed in nice clothes—at least she wore matching colors and patterns, which I thought was a dead giveaway, considering the kind of outfits some of my first-grade cohorts showed up in.

But as I discovered in the disappointing outcome with Dorrie, appearances can be deceiving. Her family wasn't low class, by any means. They lived only a few blocks from us and were respectable, hardworking folks. They just weren't quite part of our social circle. Add to that Dorrie's disability, which made other people uncomfortable with her, and my mother's judgment of her being "not the right kind of people" was sealed.

Gradually I learned. By the time I was in junior high, I could spot White Trash in a millisecond. White Trash kids had dirty fingernails, regularly spoke in ungrammatical constructions, and wore the same clothes every day. Working Class kids wore the same clothes every week, rode the school bus, and carried brown-bag lunches to the cafeteria. Middle Class kids whose parents both worked rode their bikes to school and had keys to the house.

I learned, all right—but the problem was, I didn't care. As much as I wanted to please Mama, to make her proud, my mind kept dragging me back to the nagging issue of character.

It was the school's fault. Here I was, a Bell, of the Clarksville Bells, thrown in with people of every imaginable class and background. What was I supposed to think when I met a girl like Lorene Clay, from the wrong side of the tracks—the wittiest, funniest, most intelligent girl in the sixth grade? Or a boy like Jay-Jay Dickens—poor as a churchmouse but nevertheless a perfect gentleman, with the soul of a poet—who defended my honor when the boys with a Good Name and a Good Heritage tried to get their jollies groping me in the hall between classes?

How was I supposed to respond when the people I connected with, heart and soul and mind, were not people who would make Mama proud?

After Mama left to get her hair done, I wrote all of this in my journal. Another piece to the puzzle of what it meant to be a Bell woman.

"Blood will tell," my mother always said. But the only thing blood told me was that I wanted nothing whatsoever to do with the Thorntons and the Van-Burens and the McKennas and the rest of the cretins whose names rendered them suitable companions for a girl who bore the honored name of Bell. Instead, I found my place among the unwashed multitudes, those ordinary people who had no name, no connections, no country club membership—nothing to recommend them except nobility of soul and integrity of heart.

Thus, in the glorious, liberated hours between eight and three, I lived surrounded by a circle of friends who made me laugh, made me think, and ultimately forced me to accept myself by the sheer compelling power of their classless, unconditional acceptance.

I had learned my lesson from the debacle with Dorrie Meacham—but not the precept my mother intended to teach me. I didn't avoid developing friendships with people like Lorene Clay and Jay-Jay Dickens. In fact, I gave myself to them with an emotional vulnerability unbecoming a Southern Lady. I laid down the power of my name, opened my secrets to them without shame, and learned to love and be loved without reservation.

I just never brought them home.

· 9 ·

I never brought Charles Chase home, either, but for an entirely different reason.

Under better circumstances, Charles might have been just the kind of man you'd bring home to meet your mama. He was sweet and considerate and down-to-earth; cute, but not handsome enough to raise suspicion; and although I knew next to nothing about him, he seemed like a pretty upstanding guy.

I wondered, though.

We mostly met at the cabin out on the river, which made up in privacy what it lacked in ambience. I assumed he had taken the fishing camp as his primary residence after the separation from his wife, but I could have been wrong. We never talked about it.

We never talked about anything.
We just . . . well, you know.

Maybe this is why people are attracted to the idea of having affairs. There are no complications, none of the dull, ordinary stuff that gets in the way. No socks on the floor or empty toilet paper rolls, no baskets of laundry or smelly gym shorts.

Just pure (or rather, impure) sex. The giddiness of romance without the weight of reality.

The problem is, I like reality. Despite the pain I've gone through with Robert's rejection, I find myself still wanting the normal stuff—the dailyness of life shared with another human being, the conversation, the challenges, the easy laughter, the inside jokes, the memories that build, one by one, into a history.

I want commitment.

I just don't want it with Charles Chase.

There was nothing wrong with Charles, except that he obviously did not care about having a relationship. He wanted an affair. He occasionally took me out for elaborate and expensive dinners in Tupelo and Tuscaloosa, places where no one would recognize us. He bought me flowers and, once, a small gold heart on a chain. He told me I was beautiful and opened doors for me and treated me as if I were royalty.

But he never said, "I love you."

*   *   *

Love.

Now, there's a subject big enough to keep every therapist in the nation rolling in dough. Especially if the client in question has been brought up to be a Southern Lady.

Let's put aside for the moment the silver screen's steamy images of the sexuality of Southern women—Natalie Wood in *Splendor in the Grass*, for example, or Elizabeth Taylor in *Cat on a Hot Tin Roof.* Southern women are not taught to enjoy sex. Southern women are coached to use sex to gain and maintain power.

All right, I'll admit it—it's a generalization. Some Southern women probably do enjoy sex and have fruitful, fulfilling intimate lives with their chosen mates or whoever else strikes their fancy. But the Bell women, from Great-great-great-grandma Alberta right down to the present, saw more potential in copulation than merely a method of reproduction or an afternoon delight.

All Southern mothers read out of the same Bible. The first commandment is: "Make your mama proud, now." The second is like unto it: "Good girls don't."

It's sort of an all-purpose principle that can be applied in a variety of situations. Good girls don't smoke—or if they do smoke, they don't do it standing up or on the street or any place where the preacher might see. Good girls don't drink—or if they do drink, they order up a feminine buzz like a pink lady or a fuzzy navel, and always in moderation. Good girls don't get drunk—or if they do get drunk, they do so in the privacy of their own boudoir, not out in public.

Good girls don't do a lot of things. But most important, good girls don't have premarital (or extramarital, or nonmarital) sex. On the other hand, if they do have premarital sex, good girls don't get pregnant. And . . . if they do get pregnant, good girls don't let the bastard get away without paying for it.

The Southern Lady's approach to sex can be very confusing for an adolescent whose hormones are beginning to assert themselves. Just as I was entering puberty, Mama started trying to give me "the talk."

As if I didn't already know where babies came from. After all, my best friend, Lorene Clay, was the oldest of seven children. The most recent two babies had been born at home, with Lorene assisting. In addition, the bedroom Lorene shared with two of her sisters was only a paper-thin wall away from her parents' room.

She told me how she would lie awake at night and listen to them generating the next little Clay offspring—a process punctuated with moans and groans and repeated prayers of "Oh, God!" (the Clays were apparently a very religious family) and culminating in a shuddering creak of the old iron bed. She had even seen them doing it once, during the year her father was unemployed, one afternoon when she came home from school early with a stomachache. Apparently she had watched for a long time, terrified at the primal energy but fascinated by her mother's agility and her father's endurance. She had described the incident in graphic detail.

No wonder my mother didn't want me associating with White Trash.

Mama's "talk" with me omitted most of the more salient particulars I had picked up from Lorene Clay. Mama explained what was happening to my body— she called it "the curse"—and how I would have to put up with this inconvenience every month of my life until I got really old, maybe forty or fifty, and then it went away. In the meantime, as long as I was getting my Monthly Visitor, it was possible for me to have a baby.

A woman became a mother, Mama said, when her husband "took his pleasure" with her. Without ever using a single anatomically correct term, she got the basic information across about how this happened. But the more important message she wanted to convey was how a Southern Lady dealt with this anomaly, this strange ritual of human mating.

First, Mama emphasized, a Southern Lady never, never does it until she is married. Something about buying the cow and giving away the milk for free. I didn't understand the bovine analogy, but I did know she wasn't telling the truth. As far back as Great-great-

great-grandma Alberta, Bell women had done it before marriage. GiGi told me so—or at least implied it. Otherwise how would Alberta have had the leverage to force Adolphus Bell to marry her?

Second, Mama said, once a Southern Lady is married, she only does it with her husband, and at his initiation. "Marital obligation," she called it, which left me with the distinct impression that engaging in sex was rather like scrubbing the kitchen floor—not high on a woman's list of desirable activities but necessary for the maintenance of a proper home. Something you did once a week whether it needed doing or not.

Once she was satisfied that I understood the basics, Mama launched into a diatribe entitled "What Men Want." This diatribe was only superficially concerned with the issue of male libido—it was, at base, a primer on the Southern Lady's control of the phallus.

"Men have certain urges, Priscilla," my mother said. "Urges that drive them to want . . . well, what they want. We women have more discretion, and a true Southern Lady, if she is wise, will employ those powers of restraint where physical intimacy is concerned."

Translation: When you've got a guy by the family jewels, you can get just about anything your deceptive little heart desires.

My mother didn't know it, but I had already seen the principle in action. I had, on certain occasions, watched her subtle interchanges with my father, how she would spurn his romantic overtures with a word or a disdainful glance, only to turn around and play up to him when she wanted something from him. It was a delicate dance, this waltz of rejection and desire. Seduction, even within the holy bonds of matrimony, was a woman's most effective means of exercising control.

And control—particularly in sexual matters—was the operative word for a Southern Lady.

"It is the girl's responsibility to say no," Mama emphasized. "You can't count on a boy—even a properly brought up Southern boy—to behave like a gentleman. The girl has to set the standard and hold to it."

Even as an adolescent I was aware, in a vague way, of how patently unfair this system was—unfair to the boy as well as to the girl. On the one hand, the girl had to be the one to "set the standard," as Mama put it, always taking responsibility for guarding her virginity. On the other hand, a girl could use whatever sexual wiles were at her disposal to make a boy desire her, only to put the brakes on and leave him frustrated to the point of acceding to her every whim. The ultimate whim, of course, being the long trip down the aisle.

Once the nuptials had been accomplished, however, the rules of the game changed. The girl was now free to say yes—in fact, she was duty bound to say yes. She was expected, on the wedding night, to throw off years of restraint and conditioning and surrender to her groom with open arms, to sacrifice her virginity upon the altar of marital obligation. But she shouldn't expect to enjoy her newfound liberty. Instead, she was instructed to lie back and let him "have his pleasure" at her expense. Her consolation prizes for this gesture of generosity were a diamond—preferably one much larger than he could afford—a house, a car, a regular income, perhaps a baby or two, and a whole new social circle of other friends who were Happily Married.

Before the wedding, according to my mother, a Southern Lady withheld the ultimate sexual favor in exchange for a gold band—in short, she remained chaste in order to be chased. After the eligible mate "chased her until she caught him," she then bartered the Act for other goods and services.

It sounded perfectly horrible to me—a covert prostitution, sanctified by holy vows and whitewashed by a lace dress with seed pearls. I didn't want anything to do with it. Ever.

But of course I didn't tell my mother that. For a Southern Lady, the only thing worse than having a promiscuous daughter was having a single one. If your daughter turned up pregnant, you could explain to your friends how the poor girl had been taken advantage of by some smooth-talking cad. Or—if the boy in question was socially acceptable marriage material—you could spring for a hurry-up wedding before she got too far along for the white dress. You could weep happy crocodile tears at the service, as if your friends didn't know the truth. And then you could boast about her incredible good fortune when the eight-pound "premature" grandbaby came along six months later.

But you couldn't, under any circumstances, give justifiable cause for a daughter who chose to remain single, have a career, and live on her own. A daughter who refused to play the game by any rules. Virginity was a prize to be guarded, but only up to a certain point. Beyond that, well, people might talk. And if they came around to whispering the L word behind their hands, the poor mother might as well slit her wrists and put herself out of her misery.

Mama never said it outright, but she made perfectly clear what my responsibility as a Southern Lady was: first to say "No," then to say "I do," and finally to say "Yes." Within the bounds of reason, of course, and when it suited my purposes.

Good girls didn't. Unless they had something to gain.

Unless they had something to gain. . . .

That was exactly what I was taught, although Mama would never have admitted it, never in a hundred lifetimes.

The larger question was, what did I hope to gain with Charles Chase? I was a grown woman, capable of making her own decisions, no longer ruled by the expectations of others. What did I get out of this affair with Charles that kept me coming back for more?

Not love, certainly. He quite deliberately avoided using the word, perhaps in a misguided effort not to lead me on. It wasn't sex, either, because although I'm quite capable of enjoying the experience, I'm also old enough and, I hope, wise enough to realize that physical intimacy is only a small component of the much larger picture.

No, it was something else. Something I couldn't name.

Or something I didn't want to name.

There was the white-haired old fool again, buzzing in my ear: *Everything you need is already within you. You have the insight. You know the answer. Find it. Seek it out. Let it rise to the surface of your consciousness.*

Maybe he was right. Maybe the truth was within me. But I wasn't going to dredge it up now. I was pretty well exhausted, and I still had to get ready to meet Charles at seven.

I'd take a page out of Scarlett's book and think about it tomorrow.

After all, tomorrow is another day.

· 10 ·

Tomorrow.

You always think you can deal with things tomorrow, until the new day dawns bearing bad news. Until it shows up with an unanticipated change of direction that jerks a knot into every preconceived notion you had about how things were going to be.

There is no tomorrow. Only today. Only right now.

"Living in the present" might seem like a worthy goal, but only if the present is worth living in.

It's time for a change. It's time for God or the universe or somebody to give me a break. I don't want to live this way anymore.

I looked down at the words and felt as if someone else had written them:

I don't want to live this way anymore.

Those were the exact words Charles Chase used last night when he broke it off. He was going back to his wife, he said, to try to work things out. I had helped him see the truth about himself, helped him become a better man, and he would always be grateful.

And he had finally uttered the L word—*love*. Only not in reference to me.

Was this the way my life was destined to be? Forty-five and single, a former beauty queen gone to seed and headed downhill, abandoned by those who claimed to love her— or at least want her?

I don't want to live this way anymore.

I read the sentence over and over again, prodded by that niggling awareness that comes with years of therapy—the knowledge that something I'd read or heard or taken out of context was exactly the insight I needed, if I could just find the way to apply it.

I could envision my therapist peering at me over the top of his glasses, smiling, eager. Waiting for the moment of revelation that would validate his existence and change me forever.

I stared at the sentence until my eyes burned, as if the words might suddenly shift and morph into something different, a coded message that held all the answers in the universe. But no doorway opened up to the world beyond. No magic happened. Just blue ink on a white page in neat, even handwriting.

Without so much as a warning knock, the bedroom door opened. I slammed the journal shut and looked up. Mama, dressed to the nines in a white linen suit and lavender silk blouse, raked me up and down with a steely gaze.

"The service," she said, "begins in thirty minutes."

Service? I had no idea what she was talking about. And then it hit me. Sunday. It was Sunday, and Mama expected me to go to church with her.

Sheesh. I got to my feet and ran a hand through my hair, and for a fleeting moment I considered the possibility of doing exactly what Mama expected me to do—rush around to get ready, dress up . . .

I don't want to live this way anymore.

I sat back down on the bed. "Thanks anyway, Mama, but I think I'll pass on church this morning."

She stared at me as if I'd grown a third eye. "Excuse me?"

"I'm just going to stay here—make some breakfast, sit on the verandah. Do a little journaling." I held up the brown leather book.

"Young lady—"

"Mama, I do not want to go to church this morning.

I don't know why you want to go, for that matter. You've told me a hundred times how much you despise this new minister."

"That's beside the point."

"What is the point, then?"

"The point is," Mama said, "you go to church because it's the right thing to do."

I wanted to ask, *Right for whom?* But I left it alone, and when she realized I wasn't going to budge on the issue, Mama abandoned me to my sin and went on to worship without me.

I made a fresh pot of coffee, took my journal out to the back verandah, and began to reflect on religion.

Mama is mistaken. Or deluded.

Maybe for some, churchgoing is about doing right. But for others, it's about appearing to *be* right.

All Southerners claim to be Christians. They can turn fire hoses on a civil rights demonstration or spend Saturday night wearing a white sheet, drinking corn liquor, and burning crosses in the front yards of black and Jewish community leaders, but come Sunday morning, they are spiffed up in their finest, warming the family pew and singing gospel songs.

In the South, being a Christian—and a regular churchgoer—is an important statement about your values. You can't get elected dogcatcher, never mind mayor or senator or governor, without at least one photo shoot on the steps of a church, with a big black Bible in one hand and the other wrapped around your smiling wife and children. Whether you ever open that Bible or give a second thought to its teachings is beside the point. As long as you're a professing Christian it doesn't matter if you're a practicing atheist. It's the image that counts.

I stared at the page, wondering where such cynicism had come from. I believed in God, prayed on occasion, and liked Jesus a lot. At least I liked the earthy, human Jesus who roamed the pages of the gospels, preaching love and healing folks and touching lepers and gathering in the outcasts. I had to admit I didn't much care for the other Jesus, the judgmental one who seemed to hover around conservative pulpits these days, separating sheep from goats and making sure the wrong people didn't get in through the narrow gate.

Right now I could have used a good dose of that first Jesus. Someone, anyone, who would see me for myself, who would love me and accept me unconditionally, without criticism, without expecting some monumental transformation.

Back toward Main Street, carillon bells rang out on the morning air. It was First Methodist; it had the sweetest bells in Chulahatchie. I put down my pen and I listened for a while, the tune as familiar to me as my own name:

"Come home, come home . . . ye who are weary, come home. . . ."

The music seeped into my soul and triggered a long-buried memory.

Homecoming.

One year in late spring—I was perhaps eight or nine—we took a trip back to Tennessee, to Bell Cove Presbyterian, out in the country near Clarksville, for what Mama called a "homecoming."

"Homecoming" at Bell Cove Pres was less a church gathering than a family reunion for the Bell clan. "This is part of your heritage, Priscilla," Mama told me with pride. "This is our church."

By "our church," she didn't mean the congregation we belonged to and attended on a more or less regular basis. The Tennessee Bells didn't belong to the church; the church belonged to them. Bell Cove Presbyterian had, quite literally, been owned by the Bell family and its heirs, well into the twentieth century.

The original Bells had built the sanctuary themselves, right on the Bell Plantation, using slave labor and hand-fired bricks. The Bells held the deed to the land and the building. The Bells made the decisions about what would transpire within the church's walls—right down to Bell approval for each new minister, and the vote condemning one hapless organist to unemployment because he was suspected of being what my grandmother GiGi called a fancy man. "Queer fingers," she said, "have no place on a Bell organ."

The Bell family—which meant my great-grandmother and her sisters, along with GiGi and her cousins—had held on to ownership of Bell Cove Presbyterian until the eleventh hour, when pressure from the national presbytery at last prevailed. In 1935 the building had finally been released, with great reluctance, to presbytery control, but not before it had been placed on the National Register of Historic Places and marked with a huge plaque in honor of the original Bell family and their offspring.

My first glimpse of the ancient house of worship brought a swell of pride to my childish heart, pride that was quickly replaced with confusion. It was a rectangular building of red brick, with a wide front porch and square white columns. A simple, elegant, thoroughly Southern church, but with one baffling feature. High on the upper level, where a second-story verandah might have been, hung two narrow white doors. No steps, no way to get up there. Just doors, closed and locked.

I drew my father aside and asked him what they were for. In the old days, he told me, there had been a balcony in the church, now long since torn down, and outside stairs leading up to the mysterious doors. "That's where the slaves went in for church," he explained. Into the balcony from the outside of the building, with no access to the main sanctuary.

He said it with pride, as if the Bells, in allowing their Negroes into the building at all, had struck some kind of primal blow for civil rights. All I could think of was how eerie the doors looked, hanging there in midair like they had been lynched and left to die.

No black faces joined the worship that homecoming Sunday, although I heard a few of the ladies talking, as they spread a feast on the tables that lined the tree-shaded grounds, of how their "girls" had labored all week to produce these pies and cakes and fried chicken and casseroles. After dinner, while the women gossiped and the men pitched horseshoes, I wandered out back, down the hill behind Bell Cove Presbyterian, where the cemetery dated to the early eighteen hundreds.

I saw my family's name on nearly every tombstone: Claudia Stone Bell, who died at age four of scarlet fever. Ronald William Bell, of the First Tennessee Regiment, who fought bravely in the conflict and expired at age twenty from the wounds of war. And smaller markers, too, in the perimeter among the weeds: Sassy and Marcus, Brownie and Rooster Joe. And one that struck me with the force of a physical blow: Little Peach.

I don't know how long I stood there, staring at that weathered stone with its two simple words. I don't know how many times Mama had to shout down the hill before I heard her, calling that the homemade ice cream was ready and I should stop being antisocial and come play with my cousins.

All I could hear, in the breeze that rustled through the cedar trees around the cemetery, were the low echoes of Negro spirituals, rising on the wind. Slave music, the kind of songs Molly-Faith Johnston sang in my grandmother's kitchen as she went about her work and planted within me the suspicion that I might be linked to her by blood as well as heart. Songs of a faith that I knew, instinctively, went deeper than my mother's concept of religion as social acceptability. Songs of hope. Songs of freedom. Music long silenced at Bell Cove Presbyterian by those tiny, weatherworn markers in the church cemetery.

Someday I would learn those songs and sing them for myself.

Someday.

Mama mighta been the one in the pew, but I think I was the one who went to church. Right there in my striped pajamas on the back verandah, drinking coffee and writing in my journal.

Until I wrote it, I hadn't remembered all that about Bell Cove Presbyterian and the cemetery and my feelings about seeing my name on a slave child's tombstone.

I'd forgotten a lot, it seemed. Being back at Belladonna stirred the pot and brought up all sorts of memories. Memories and dreams and longings I'd pushed down or covered up or lost along the way. I had lived my life the way Mama expected, trying to please her, trying to be the person she wanted me to be. Then I married Robert and simply adopted his set of standards and expectations.

I flipped back a few pages and reread the words I didn't understand:

I don't want to live this way anymore.

Something moved inside me—a seismic shift of the heart, an invisible earthquake—and at last I understood. I had never declared my own emancipation. Not from Mama. Not from Robert. Not from my own spinelessness.

In forty-five years I had never sung those freedom songs for myself. Not a single note.

And it was about damn time.

PART TWO

Unfolding

. . .

How do I know what I think
until I've written it?

How do I know
what I believe
except by trial and error,
exploration
and discovery?

How do I know myself
until I find the courage
to break open my soul
and be known
by another?

Spring came and went, and by the time June rolled around, it was clear we were in for a sweltering Mississippi summer. The kind I hadn't missed one bit since moving to the more temperate climes of the Blue Ridge.

My mother was not at all pleased with my newfound emancipation. Not that I expected her to be. I had given up makeup and taken to roaming around town in old cut-off blue jeans and ancient T-shirts. Looking, in Mama's words, like some middle-aged hippie, showing her toes in sandals—but, Lord have mercy, no pedicure.

"For heaven's sake, Priscilla," Mama said, "would it kill you to fix up a bit? Just a little dab of lipstick, even. Don't you care what people think?"

Fact was, I didn't. For the first time in my life, I wasn't

concerned about my appearance, my image, or other people's approval or disapproval. And it was incredibly liber-
ating.

"What difference does it make?" I said. "Nobody rec-
ognizes me anyway."

"Now, that's God's honest truth," Mama muttered
under her breath.

She left for her bridge club without saying another
word, but I knew what she was thinking. I was Priscilla
Rondell, golden child of Chulahatchie, the beautiful little
girl who had grown up to be Soybean Queen, Miss Ole
Miss, and second runner-up to Miss Mississippi. Besides
that, I was a Bell of the Tennessee Bells, and a Bell woman
would sooner go out in public as naked as Lady Godiva
than be seen without her face and hairdo intact.

When the door shut behind her, I exhaled relief. I
had survived these months by keeping my distance from
Mama, and she from me. We had settled into an uneasy
truce: I had no place else to go, and she had no one else to
criticize.

Mama and me—the perfect dovetailing of neuroses.
Each morning we go our own ways, and each evening
we sit down to supper and sparring.

Or so I'd like to think, if I could rewrite history to
suit myself. The closer truth is, she strikes, and I turn
the other cheek. Just as I've always done.

Why can't I stand up for myself? Wearing cutoffs and T-shirts isn't exactly taking a stand. It's simply pushing her buttons. It irritates the hell out of her, and I know it, so I do it. But it doesn't make me more of an adult, more of an equal (as "sparring" would imply).

How did I get here? Where did this habit of submission come from? It's not my nature—or at least it doesn't feel like my nature. Yet when I look at my relationships, not just with Mama but with everybody close to me, I can't deny that I've spent my life trying to please.

Trying, and failing.

Trying harder, and failing more spectacularly.

This was exactly the kind of self-examination my old fool of a therapist had hoped for, exactly what he'd applaud. And so, perversely, I didn't give him the satisfaction. During our weekly telephone session, I hemmed and hawed and mumbled when he asked what I'd been learning, and then I listened to him go on and on about how important it was for me to be using this time to full advantage. For eleven solid minutes he ranted, practically without taking a breath.

I timed him, and later I deducted it from my check.

I'd been holding on by my fingernails for months, all the way through the spring and summer, and I was sick and tired of it all. Sick and tired of being stuck here with Mama on my back all the livelong day. Sick and tired of hearing what a disappointment I was. Sick and tired of feeling like a failure with no hope and no prospects.

Sick and tired of being sick and tired.

I need for something to happen, I wrote in my journal. *Something. Anything.*

And then something did.

· 12 ·

The Heartbreak Cafe wasn't the kind of restaurant Mama would set foot in, not if her hair was on fire and that battered aluminum water pitcher held the last douse left on the face of the earth.

And to be perfectly candid, it was the lack of Mama that made the diner nearly perfect.

The cafe was pretty much what you'd expect from the name—not dismal, exactly, but certainly, ah, *vintage*. Or at least that was the impression the place gave off when you initially walked in. Once you got used to it, it wasn't so bad, really. It smelled deliciously of bacon and coffee and cinnamon apples. Not fancy, by any stretch of the imagination, but scrubbed and bright and healthy feeling. A clean, well-lighted place.

* * *

"A Clean, Well-Lighted Place."

I remember studying that short story years ago, back in college. Hemingway. His stripped-down prose made everything in life seem somehow stark and drear, like razor-sharp photographic images in black-and-white. This particular story's about an old drunk man, if I'm remembering correctly, who tried to commit suicide and failed, and now has nowhere else to go for solace but this small cafe, this "clean, well-lighted place."

Sheesh. There's a metaphor for you. A narrow and tragic universe, marked by suffering so profound that it goes unnoticed—or at least unremarked upon.

Perhaps I should toss that out and see what the old white-haired fool thinks of it.

Meanwhile, I'm grateful for some space away from Belladonna and from Mama. Here in this booth, I have the best of both worlds. I can be with people without actually having to interact with them. The semblance of relationship without any of the demands.

That doesn't sound very emotionally healthy, as I'm sure the old shrink would be quick to point out, but I'm supposed to be honest here and not simply try to make myself look good (for whom?). And the truth is, after the fiasco with Charles Chase, I'm none too eager for any kind of relationship at the moment.

Was it a fiasco? I keep asking myself that question.

Did it have a purpose—other than the obvious, which was to let me bask for a while in the ephemeral delusion that I'm still attractive and desirable?

He hasn't called me. I tried to call him a few times, but he wasn't answering his cell. I didn't leave a message.

I can't figure out if I really miss him or if I only miss the concept of him. The idea of someone who might rouse from the lethargy of a self-absorbed universe to care whether I was alive. Whether I was happy or not.

Once or twice I drove out past the river camp but saw no signs of life. I have to conclude that he went back to his wife, and in my better moments I wish him well and hope he's been able to patch things up. On my less noble days I'd just like to feel the comfort of some human contact. Skin. His, or anyone else's, for that matter—

"Want a refill, Peach?"

I slammed the journal shut and jerked to attention. My heart pounded like a thunder drum. It was that woman, the one with salt-and-pepper hair and a perpetually ragged look around her eyes. She was the owner of the place, I was pretty sure. At least she was always here, she and the big black man whose name seemed to be Scratch.

And she had called me by name.

"Excuse me?" I muttered.

She held up the pot. "I asked if you'd like more coffee."

"Oh, yes. Thanks." I pushed my mug over toward the edge of the table. "Do we know each other?"

"It's Chulahatchie, hon. Everybody knows everybody." She grinned. "To be more precise, everybody knows *you*. You're the closest thing we've got to a celebrity, and—"

She saw something on my face, something I wasn't hiding very well, and stopped short. "Sorry. I'm Dell Haley. I own this place." She grinned. "Well, technically I lease it and the Chulahatchie Savings and Loan owns it. But it's still mine, long as I pay the bills."

"Nice to meet you, Dell." I held out a hand. She set down the coffeepot, swiped her palm across her apron, and shook it.

"I was married by the time you started high school," she said, "but I reckon you remember Boone Atkins." She pointed.

He slid out of his booth and came in my direction, and all I could think was, *Wow*.

"Hey, Peach," he said. "Welcome home."

He leaned against the booth on Dell's side and stood there with a relaxed, easy grace. My gut lurched with a little electric shock when he put his hand on her shoulder, as if the gesture was so familiar as to be unconscious.

Could the two of them be—?

Nah, not possible. She had to be ten years older than him.

"You've got a Dorian Gray portrait hidden in your closet somewhere," I told him. "You look exactly the same."

"So do you, Peach," he said. "I'm glad to see you."

It was a lie, of course, but what a gracious, compassionate lie! Here I sat, forty pounds overweight, in jeans and a tattered Ole Miss sweatshirt with the sleeves cut off—no makeup, looking like something the cat dragged in.

We chatted, made a little small talk, and he went on his way. But I could not get him out of my mind, standing there, gazing down at me with those gorgeous eyes, bringing back one of the sweetest, bitterest memories of my adolescence.

Lord help me, how could I forget? Boone Atkins—tenderhearted, gorgeous, the only boy besides Jay-Jay who ever treated me like a real person with a brain and a heart and a soul. Oh, yes, I remembered Boone. Boone was the one who saved me. And he never even knew it.

Midway through the eighth grade, Jay-Jay Dickens's daddy got transferred to Oklahoma. Or at least that's what he told folks. The whole truth (as only Lorene and I knew it) was that Mr. Dickens had lost his job and couldn't support his family, so they were all moving west to live with his aunt and uncle in Enid.

Lorene and I watched as they loaded their belongings into Jay-Jay's daddy's pickup truck until it looked like the Okies leaving the Dust Bowl, or the Clampetts on their way to Beverly Hills. The only thing missing was Granny's rocking chair on top of the pile.

We said our good-byes and left as night was falling.

The next morning at school the rumor spread like flesh-eating bacteria: Jay-Jay's daddy had gone and killed himself. He'd put a bullet through his head by wrapping his mouth around the barrel of a twelve-gauge shotgun and pulling the trigger with his big toe.

Without a word to anyone, Lorene and I left school and hightailed it over to Jay-Jay's house. The sheriff's car was just driving away when we showed up.

"So it's true, then," I said, but looking at Jay-Jay's face I hadn't really needed to ask the question.

He nodded. His eyes seemed blank and unfocused.

"What are you going to do now?" It was a stupid question, but I had to fill the empty spaces somehow, try to get closer to him, try to draw him back.

He shrugged. "Go on to Enid, I reckon. Can't stay here, anyhow."

I opened my mouth to argue with him and then realized the truth of what he said. For one thing, their little rental house had a new tenant coming in next week. But even more important, staying in Chula-hatchie would mean living forever with the shame and scandal of his father's suicide.

Three days later, we stood on the banks of the Tombigbee River and watched as Mr. Dickens's ashes floated downstream on the surface of the brown water, around the bend and out of sight. Mrs. Dickens looked pale and rawboned and dazed as she climbed behind the wheel of the pickup and waved good-bye. Jay-Jay waved, too, from his spot in the passenger's seat, his jaw set in a rigid line and his eyes narrowed with determination. But he didn't cry. He had to be strong, had to take care of his mama. The note his daddy left him told him so—the same note that explained about the life insurance and how they'd be taken care of now and never have to worry about anything.

Jay-Jay Dickens was fourteen the day he became a man.

His daddy never knew that his life insurance ran out the minute he got fired. Or that it didn't cover suicide.

The day after Jay-Jay left, I went back to school. Everybody was talking about it, and everybody knew I was Jay-Jay's friend. They came to me for the gory details: Had I seen the body? Was there blood everywhere? Who found the corpse? Was it Jay-Jay?

They circled like a pack of hounds scenting blood. Snarling, snapping, closing in.

"Leave her alone."

The voice, calm and quiet and assured, silenced the mob as if they'd all been struck dumb on the spot. Boone Atkins faced them down, all of them. Shut them up and scattered them like chaff to the winds. Took my hand and found a deserted classroom, where we skipped third period and sat for over an hour—just sitting, saying nothing. When I cried he held my hand but didn't try to talk me out of feeling sad.

With Boone, I didn't have to be anything special. Didn't have to put on an act or play the beauty queen or stifle my tears because they'd make my eyes all bloodshot and my nose runny.

I could just be myself.

I don't think I ever thanked him for that gift.

· 13 ·

There were other gifts from Boone as well.

No one would ever take Jay-Jay's place in my life. But suddenly Boone Atkins was there, appearing out of thin air like an illusionist, expanding to fill at least some of the empty space.

I make it sound as if Jay-Jay was the one who died. That's how it felt, even though I got the occasional letter from him trying to convince me how well he was doing. He and his mama arrived in Oklahoma just as the oil boom of the eighties was getting off the ground.

He quit school, went to work with his uncle on the rigs, made a little money, and invested it ten years later in a small business. A cousin who went to school at Stanford knew a couple of guys working on a computer program they called BackRub.

Later known as Google.

Jay-Jay did all right for himself, at least in terms of material success. But somehow it all seemed rather sad to me. He was so smart, and so kind, and so compassionate, but he never went back to finish his education. And I wonder how much of the kindness was kicked out of him in the rough world of wildcatting.

I suspect something of Jay-Jay did die with his father that night. His hope, perhaps. His optimism. His dreams.

You'da thought Mama would be glad to see Jay-Jay go. She never met him face-to-face, but she heard me talk about him now and again, and I knew without even bothering to ask that Jay-Jay Dickens was not "our kind of people."

The problem was, neither was Boone. He came from a nice family, but that didn't matter to Mama. She didn't care a lick that he was handsome and polite and smart and treated others with respect. His folks didn't have much in the way of money, but that wasn't the primary issue. He was the subject of gossip, and that alone was enough for Mama.

"He's not right," she said every time I raised the issue.

"But, Mama—"

"Don't 'but, Mama' me," she said. "Trust me, Priscilla, the boy's not right."

"You've never even met him!"

"As long as you live under my roof, young lady, you will abide by my wishes."

Lord, if I'd heard that sentence once, I'd heard it a thousand times. She didn't see me mocking her, mimicking the words behind her back, and it was a good thing, too. It might've been the last lip sync of my short but remarkable life.

Dating.

The male of the species tends to view this ritual as a hunt—stalking the elusive prey, cutting out the best and most beautiful of the herd, narrowing down the field, and then, by superior wit and cunning, following at a distance until the chosen one steps daintily into the net. But for a Southern girl being schooled toward Southern Lady–hood, dating is an extended shopping trip where all manner of potential mates are tried on for compatible color, fit, style, and size.

After my mother gave me "the talk," my father— who usually stayed out the way and left my education in Mama's capable hands—came forward to add one bit of wisdom to the mix. "Peach, honey," he said, "I would never advise a daughter of mine to marry for money. But remember, it is just as easy to fall in love with a rich man as it is to give your heart to a pauper."

My mother clarified Daddy's advice with a metaphor of her own: "If you're looking for a designer dress, Priscilla, you don't shop at Kmart."

I understood what was expected of me. As much as it galled my fifteen-year-old soul, I accepted an invitation to attend the sophomore class dance with William Robeson McKenna III, the eldest son of my father's law partner. We were to double-date with Sarah Thornton and her boyfriend, Walter Stubblefield.

I had known Sarah, of course, since we were in elementary school, and I didn't like her any better by this point than I had when she bullied Dorrie Meacham on the playground in first grade. She was still a bully, although a much more refined and elegant bully, but she was the daughter of one of Daddy's richest clients, so I had to endure her company more often than I would have liked—which was never.

Walter, who was sixteen and had both a driver's license and a brand-new convertible, thought he was hot stuff. At school Sarah hung on him as if she were sliding off the deck of the *Titanic* and he was her only lifeline. Perhaps he was. Sarah, after all, provided living proof of the great high school dichotomy, that the most popular girl in school—that is, the one who ends up being cheerleader, homecoming queen, and most sought-after prom date—is often the least liked person in three counties.

I had two viable offers for my first date—not bad,

considering that I was known as the Pageant Princess, and in terms of approachability might as well have been a six-foot-four African supermodel. Most boys were too terrified to come within spitting distance.

I was also too smart for my own good.

Southern girls learn early that if they're bright, they'd better put their candle under a bushel, and fast. Boys aren't attracted to intelligent girls, Mother told me, but by the time she got around to imparting this gem of wisdom, it was too late. I knew better. What boys weren't attracted to was girls who intimidated them. They wanted to feel superior, even if they had to get the sensation under false pretenses. And of course a well-trained young Southern Lady let them have their illusion of supremacy and used it to her own advantage.

Besides all that, my friends weren't "the right kind of people." Sarah once warned me, in that snotty, holier-than-thou tone of hers, that I'd better dump the trash if I expected to be taken seriously.

If truth be told, I would have rather gone to the dance with Boone, but given that impossibility, I chose the lesser of two evils. Robbie McKenna was at least good-looking and had nice eyes, even if he was a wuss. The other offer had come from Marshall Threadgood, left tackle on the football team. Sarah had encouraged me to accept Marsh's grunted, monosyllabic invitation: "Want ta go ta the dance wit me?" Marsh was a rising star, she said; if I had a jock boyfriend I'd be a shoo-in for cheerleader next season.

But Marsh sat in the back row of my sophomore lit class, giving me the unfortunate opportunity to experience firsthand his lascivious perspective on selected literary giants, notably Shakespeare: "Love poems to a man, huh? I could teach him a thing or two about where to stick it." Marshall Threadgood's athletic star might have been in its ascendancy, but his brains were located at a significantly lower altitude.

Robbie McKenna, then, was the only sensible alternative—at least if I had any intention of preserving both my chastity and my sanity.

That first date set the tone for years to come.

I had chosen Robbie, whose birth and heritage should have made him a custom fit, and whose genteel manner should have been my protection. But I hadn't counted on Marshall Threadgood making obscene gestures in my direction and then picking a fight with Robbie on the dance floor. Poor Robbie tried to defend my honor, but he just didn't have the right equipment. He folded under the pressure, stepped into a right hook, and went down like a sack of black-eyed peas.

Marsh was promptly ejected from the premises, but not before the damage had been done. The paramedics came and hustled Robbie off to the emergency room to have his broken jaw wired. Sarah went to pieces and begged Walter to take her home. And as the sirens faded off into the distant night, I felt a gentle tug at my elbow.

I turned. There stood Boone Atkins, resplendent in a brand-new shiny blue suit, his gentle eyes looking me up and down.

"May I have this dance, Miss Rondell?" he asked with a low laugh. "It seems your escort has been . . . ah, temporarily incapacitated."

I took Boone's hand and followed him onto the floor. In the dim light of the Japanese lanterns strung around the gymnasium, I doubt anyone even noticed the Kmart tag that hung from a string under the armpit of his suit. I pulled it off and stuck it in my purse.

Mama was waiting at the door when Boone brought me home in his father's ten-year-old Chevrolet. Sarah's daddy had called, she said, and told them what had happened. How horrible it must have been for me, and on my first date, at that.

"I had a very nice time," I said, letting go of Boone's hand. "Mother, I don't believe you've met Boone Atkins. He was kind enough to bring me home."

"Thank you, young man, for looking after my daughter." Mother nodded formally, that icy fixed smile spreading across her lips. Her eyes traveled up to Boone's face and back down again, taking in the horrible shiny suit. But I knew she wasn't thinking about his wardrobe.

"So that's him, is it?" Mama asked scornfully as soon as the door closed behind him. "Certainly not one of our kind of people."

"He's my kind of person, Mother," I said. "He's a gentleman." With that, I left her standing in the middle of the parlor while I went to my bedroom and shut the door.

Tomorrow, no doubt, I would catch hell for associating with the likes of Boone Atkins. Tomorrow I would get a scathing lecture about a Southern Lady's responsibility for maintaining the appearance of propriety. Tomorrow things would be back to normal.

Still, it felt freeing, no matter what the outcome, to be a little more at home in my own skin, to give myself an inch or two more space to move around in. I took off my dress and hung it on the door, then emptied my purse to find the tag from Boone's precious suit. Blue Light Special—on sale, $21.95.

All through my dating years, and long after I had married Robert and left Chulahatchie, I kept that sale tag. It was my ticket to a tender memory, a reminder that not everything of value comes from Neiman Marcus.

· 14 ·

"Mind if I join you?" Boone asked.

I hadn't even heard him come over, I'd been so absorbed in writing. I shut my journal and looked up at him. He was smiling.

"Sure," I said. An unnecessary invitation, as he had already slid into the other side of the booth.

The big black man called Scratch brought more coffee and took a long time pouring it. He obviously found something amusing in the situation, because he kept looking back and forth from me to Boone, and grinning.

"What's with him?" I said when he'd gone back to the kitchen.

Boone chuckled. "He likes you."

"There's something different about him."

"What do you mean, different?"

I wasn't really sure what I meant. "It's just a feeling. Like he's hiding something."

No, that wasn't quite right.

"I don't mean *hiding*, exactly. Nothing malevolent. I just get the sense that there's more to him than meets the eye."

"There's more to everybody than meets the eye," Boone said.

He let the statement hang out there for a minute or two, gaining heft in the silence. "Take you, for instance."

"What about me?"

"Ah, now that's the great mystery."

I tried to laugh it off. "There's nothing mysterious about me."

"Oh, but there is," Boone said. "All the questions a good reporter might ask: *Who* has Peach Rondell become in the past twenty-some years? *What* does she write in that journal of hers? *Where* is that husband of hers, the college professor? *Why* does she look so sad all the time?"

He gave a self-deprecating shrug and smiled that drop-dead gorgeous smile of his, the smile that could make anybody forgive him anything, even sticking his handsome nose into someone else's personal business.

"You forgot *when*," I said.

"Ah, so I did." He rubbed the crease between his eyebrows as if deep in thought. "I've got it. *When* is Peach going to open up and trust someone to be her friend?"

I searched my brain for a lighthearted and witty comeback, but couldn't find one, and when it comes to humor,
timing is everything. Besides, my throat had clogged up
with emotion. Without warning I felt myself overtaken by
a wave of garrulousness, and I began to tell Boone Atkins
things I hadn't even told my therapist.

"When I left Chulahatchie years ago," I said, "I swore
to myself I'd never return. I'd had enough of Mama's control and manipulation. I came back once or twice for a
brief visit, just because I couldn't bear to punish Daddy for
Mama's browbeating, but I always left beaten to a bloody
pulp—at least emotionally speaking. Nothing was ever
good enough to please Mama. *I* wasn't good enough."

I paused and chanced a look up at Boone's face. He was
listening intently and nodded for me to continue.

"Anyway, I lost touch with everybody I knew growing
up." I paused, rethinking the statement. "No, that's not
right. I deliberately cut off ties with everybody. I didn't
want to be reminded of Chulahatchie, and my childhood,
and the fact that I once had been the Bean Queen and Miss
Ole Miss."

Boone chuckled as if he understood perfectly and took
a sip of his coffee.

"So when Daddy died, and I came back for the funeral,
I was a virtual stranger in my own hometown. I didn't remember anybody who showed up at the service and didn't
particularly want to make myself remember. I just flat-out
didn't care. I told my sister, Melanie, that the next time I

set foot in Mississippi, it would be to settle Mama's estate. I didn't count on—"

I stopped. How could I tell him the truth about Robert's rejection, and starting over, and my own sense of despair and worthlessness?

He mistook my hesitation for something else. "You must miss him."

Something painful twisted in my gut, like a joint turned the wrong way or the electric shock of a nerve pain. Without thinking twice, I blurted out the truth:

"I don't miss Robert," I said. "I miss feeling loved."

Boone gave me the tenderest look imaginable, and when he spoke, his voice was low, quiet, almost a whisper. "I was talking about your father," he said.

God, how stupid could I be? With one flagrant Freudian slip, I'd revealed far too much, and now I felt open and exposed as a gutted deer.

But Boone didn't seem to notice. He leaned forward and reached across the table, almost, but not quite, touching my hand. "It's okay."

"It's not okay!" I said with more passion and volume than I had intended. I lowered my voice to a hiss. "It's not okay that my husband left me for someone else and that I have no job and no source of income and no place to go. It's not okay that I've had to come back to 'visit' my mother—and yes, put it in quotation marks, because God only knows how long the visit will last before I can get back on my feet and get out of here. It's not okay that my daddy is dead and buried and no longer around when I need him. It's not okay that my life sucks and that the only person who has showed me any compassion at all was another woman's husband, and even he ended up leaving me to go back to her in the end."

Boone waited while I ground down to a stuttering halt.

"You must think I'm awful," I said.

"I don't think anything of the sort."

He pulled a wad of paper napkins out of the holder and pressed them into my hand then waited while I blew my nose.

"I think you've been hurt, and life's been difficult lately, and you don't quite know how to handle it," he said. "Chulahatchie might seem like it's still slogging through the Dark Ages, but some of us are fairly enlightened." He gave a quiet little laugh. "If you'll let us, I think you'll find some folks here who would support you."

I let the words settle and sat in silence while they echoed around inside my head. I felt strange and warm and a little frightened all at once. I'd never known this kind of acceptance, not even with Robert when we were married. And even though it came as a welcome respite, it also brought some anxiety and apprehension. If I didn't understand what I'd done to deserve it, how could I possibly know what I might do to lose it?

I tried not to think about the glass half empty. My old fool of a shrink was always talking to me about negative energy and karma and finding my center and living with an open hand. Little did he know that with Mama, if you opened your hand half an inch, whatever you had in it was going to get snatched away.

It wasn't exactly an encouraging metaphor, but God help me, it was true.

"So what do you write in that book of yours?" Boone asked.

"Just stuff," I said. "Thoughts. Memories. Ideas. When I first came back to Chulahatchie, I was sure I'd died and landed in the third circle of hell. But I've been amazed at how much I remembered that I thought I'd forgotten. I'm learning a lot about myself, gaining insight."

"If your insight about Scratch is an example, you've also got pretty good instincts about others," Boone said. "A long time ago, I remember, you said you wanted to write fiction. Maybe this is a good time to start. At the very least you'll find a lot of characters here. Maybe coming back to Chulahatchie is a blessing in disguise."

"I don't know about a blessing," I said, "but it's one heckuva good disguise."

The jury's still out on whether I believe this could be a blessing, but Boone was right about one thing: Chulahatchie sure does have more than its share of characters.

Take Scratch, for example. He's a puzzle inside an enigma wrapped in a mystery. To all appearances, he's a fry cook, busboy, and general gofer, but there's something else to that persona. Whenever I look at him—and especially when I talk to him—I get the impression of a Brooks Brothers suit disguised behind a T-shirt and apron.

If I were writing him as a character in a novel, he'd be an artist or a musician—immensely talented, but haunted by something in his past that keeps him locked inside himself. Some pain that no one understands, some hidden heartache. A love gone wrong, perhaps. A dream unfulfilled.

Every now and then you see it—the spark, the tenderness. Like when he talks to Purdy Overstreet, who's nearly lost herself to Alzheimer's. She's got a thing for Scratch; flings herself at him every time she waltzes in the door. He is always so kind with her, so gentle and understanding.

Now, Purdy is some kind of character, that's for sure. I can imagine her as somebody's little white-haired grandmother who all of a sudden had a personality transplant. She dyes her hair orange and wears miniskirts and fishnet stockings. And always a feather boa wrapped around her neck. She reminds me of Lola the showgirl in that old Barry Manilow song.

And to complete the triangle, of course, there's Hoot Everett, who might be eighty-something and toothless, but is nowhere near passionless. He's got the hots for Purdy, that much is certain. He's a love-struck puppy who can't understand why she spends all her time drooling over Scratch. If I were writing their story, the two of them would get together and prove to the world that love outlives beauty and brains and physical stamina.

I'm going to take Boone's advice, and in addition to the journaling I'm doing for therapy, I'm also going to start writing fiction. Just small stuff at first—character sketches, brief scenes. Some from observation, some from my own experience, maybe. I'll see how it feels and go from there.

What do I have to lose? I got nowhere to go and nothing but time.

And if this does turn out to be a blessing, I'll gladly eat my words—with a little butter and brown sugar, if you please.

"You're going out almost every day," Mama said.

With Mama, nothing was ever just an innocent comment. It was either a criticism or an interrogation, but always phrased so that she could claim that she meant nothing at all by it. If you took offense, it was your problem, not hers.

We were sitting on the back verandah drinking coffee in the cool of the morning. Autumn brought with it the anticipation of change—that apple-crisp snap, when the air tastes like Granny Smiths, when you can smell leaf smoke on every breeze. Fall was my favorite season, and even being in Mississippi with Mama couldn't diminish the sense of well-being that came with cooler weather. The sense of something around the bend, something exciting and challenging and—

"Priscilla, I asked you a question. Do give me the courtesy of answering."

I stifled a sigh, let go of the sense of well-being, and watched as it thinned like smoke and then vanished into nothingness.

"I didn't know there was a question on the table," I said.

Mama gave me *the look*. "I *said*—"

"I know what you said," I interrupted. "You said I'd been going out every day. That's not a question, it's a statement."

"It amounts to the same thing, and you know it," Mama said.

"If you must know, I've been hanging out at Dell Haley's diner—the Heartbreak Cafe, down on West Main."

Mama stared at me, opened her mouth, and then shut it again. She sipped her coffee and pondered. "I suppose she didn't have much choice, with her husband dying so sudden, and all."

Something jerked in my gut like a twenty-pound bass on a ten-pound test line. "Dell had a husband who died? Recently?"

"This past spring, I think. I never really knew them, not well. They weren't, ah, part of our circle. But after he died, that's when she decided to open up that dismal little cafe, I guess. Make ends meet."

For some reason I felt the need to jump in and defend Dell. "It's not dismal. The food is great. The people are nice. And she seems to be doing a booming business."

No response.

"She's been very kind to me," I went on stubbornly. "I sit in there and write, and—"

"Yes, well." Mama shrugged. "She's not your friend, Priscilla. It's her job to be nice. Just keep that in mind and don't make a nuisance of yourself."

Don't make a nuisance of yourself. Act like a lady. Make sure you're invited. Keep your own counsel. Don't get too close to the wrong kind of people.

It was just the sort of thing she might have said to me when I was four years old. My whole life long she had spoiled everything I held dear.

When was I going to learn to keep my big mouth shut and keep my treasures to myself?

15

I didn't tell my psychiatrist about Dell and Scratch and Boone Atkins and the other folks at the Heartbreak Cafe. I don't know why; perhaps the experience with Mama soured me. I didn't want him thinking I was desperate and pathetic, the way my own mother seemed to.

But if truth be told, maybe I am desperate and pathetic, I wrote in my journal. *Maybe I am a loser.*

Loser. The word I've been avoiding all these months. The word that brings me back to the part of my childhood I've intentionally repressed.

Perhaps I knew, deep down, that I wouldn't be able to avoid it forever. But hope springs eternal, as Mama used to say. Did she know the context of those lines, the way Pope originally wrote them? "Hope springs eternal in the human breast; Man never is, but always to be blest."

Lord, the old fool would love that. Not exactly a "glass half full" philosophy.

I look back through the pages I've written in the months since I returned to Mama's house, and there's so much I hadn't remembered until I began to put it all down on paper. Maybe Robert was right—maybe the umbilical cord is the primal wound inflicted by our mothers, the one that runs all the way through us to our very core. Maybe all those therapeutic stereotypes have their roots firmly in the truth of mothers and daughters.

To all external appearances, it might seem that I didn't have it so bad. My parents didn't abuse me or abandon me or neglect me. We weren't poor—just the opposite, in fact. I always had everything I needed and most of what I wanted.

Except the thing I needed and wanted most.

A mother.

From time to time various shrinks have talked to me about the principle of intermittent hope—how our psyches can be seduced by a fleeting moment of gratification into believing that a miracle has occurred, that change has come to someone we desperately want to love us. When the object of our longing reverts again to the old ways of cruelty or indifference, we cling to that shred of hope and make ourselves believe that we are loved, even with a lifetime of evidence to the contrary.

We never are, but always "to be" blessed. . . .

And somewhere along the way, we turn the finger of blame onto ourselves and call ourselves by the only names we know: Lost. Unlovable. Unworthy. Loser.

Naming is a powerful force. It defines us, charts our destiny—if not in the stars, then in our very souls.

I read and reread the words a dozen times or more as the truth sank in. Mama had named me, all right—but it wasn't the Bell name that was important. I had been named with her expectations, with her training, with her narcissism. The universe revolved around her, and I was a helpless bit of flotsam caught up in her vortex.

It didn't matter that I had taken to wearing ragged sweatshirts and no makeup and refused to go to church. That kind of outward rebellion had no effect on the inner child. Deep down, I was still a little girl who wanted and needed her mommy's approval.

"You will go through with this," Mama said.

After years of forced forgetfulness, I now remember it so clearly. Not "Are you all right, honey?" or "Do we need to go to the doctor?" but "You will go through with this."

It wasn't the first time I'd heard those words. Lord

help me, in every pageant since I was six years old, I always panicked when the spotlight came up and it was my turn to perform. I hated it, all of it—the uncomfortable dresses, the tap shoes, the curlers and makeup and hair spray. Over the years I'd made up in looks and charm what I lacked in talent, and the voice lessons Mama forced on me had paid off, at least enough that I wasn't booed off the stage. But none of this was natural for me the way it seemed to be for the other girls. The way it seemed to be for Mama.

That night, the evening of the county preliminaries for the Junior Miss Pageant, it occurred to me for the first time to wonder whether or not Mama had ever dreamed of doing this herself. Maybe she had desperately longed to be Junior Miss or Miss Mississippi, but the pageant circuit didn't come cheap, and I was pretty sure GiGi and Chick couldn't have come up with the money.

Perhaps, at sixteen, I had grown up just enough to begin seeing my mother as an individual with her own hopes and dreams and unfulfilled longings.

I was not, however, mature enough to follow that thread to its logical conclusion.

We were coming up to the final talent competition. I had been secretly hoping that someone would show up who might be my generation's version of Mary Ann Mobley, but alas, it was clear from the dismal offerings at the county level that I only had one significant competitor. Her name was Astrid, a whip-smart but socially inept girl whose talent involved a dramatic reading from the "Decree on Serfs," by Catherine the Great.

"We've got this sewn up," Mama said to me at dinner that night. "Don't eat that; it'll give you gas." She flicked a couple of broccoli florets off the top of my salad.

I toyed with the lettuce and tomato.

"Come on," Mama said. "You need to eat."

"I'm not hungry," I said. "I don't feel good."

"You don't feel well," she corrected automatically. "It's just nerves. Never mind dinner; there'll be a reception afterward."

But it wasn't just nerves. I could tell the difference. My gut was churning and I was fighting a cold sweat. By the time we got back to the auditorium, I knew I was in trouble. Big trouble. I ran for the ladies' room and barely made it, and when I came out again, Mama was consulting her watch.

"You've got fifteen minutes," she said. "Go fix your makeup."

"Mama, I'm sick." I leaned against the wall. "I don't know, it's food poisoning or something. I've got really bad diarrhea, and I feel like I'm going to throw up, too."

"You're not going to throw up," she said. "And it can't be food poisoning; we ate the same thing."

"No, we didn't. I had the Thousand Island dressing—"

She jerked me up by the elbow so hard I heard the joint pop. "It's just nerves," she said through gritted teeth. "Now, go." She shoved me in the direction of the dressing room.

I went. I patted cold water on my face and repaired my makeup. I took deep breaths. I tried to remember everything I'd ever learned about calming myself.

And then I heard the emcee: "And now, singing 'I Have Dreamed' from *The King and I*, let's give a warm welcome to Priscilla Bell Rondell, from Chulahatchie."

I headed for the stage. The accompanist had already begun my intro, and Mama had taught me how to make a sweeping, elegant entrance in time with the music. Everyone applauded. I made it to the microphone beside the grand piano.

Almost.

Bile rose up in my throat, and I fought back the gag reflex. The pianist ran through the intro a second time. It was coming, and there was nothing I could do about it. I turned on my heel and ran for the wings, where I deposited the remains of the Thousand Island dressing on the stagehand's shoes.

Someone reached for me and held me up. For a moment I thought it was Mama and envisioned a tender scene where she apologized and promised never to make me go onstage again.

But it wasn't. It was Daddy, who had dashed from his seat the moment he realized something was wrong. He held me while I retched again, ignored the stench, and rushed me off to the emergency room.

Mama never came to the hospital. She never apologized, not even when the doctor said I did have food poisoning and kept me overnight to make sure the medicine was working and I wasn't getting dehydrated. Daddy stayed, sleeping in an uncomfortable Naugahyde chair next to my bed.

The next day when we got home, Mama informed me that Astrid had taken the Serfs to victory and would be representing the county at the state Junior Miss Pageant.

Something told me Astrid didn't really need the scholarship money. Maybe her mama and mine had read out of the same book. Maybe at this very moment her mama was celebrating while Astrid was in the bathroom throwing up at the thought of having to do it all over again in front of a larger audience.

For years I tried, but I could never manage to forget what Mama said to me that day:

Priscilla, there are two kinds of people in this world—winners and losers. And I didn't bring you up to be a loser.

Naming. It's powerful. The name of Loser spurred me on to win the title of county Soybean Queen and brought me as far as second runner-up to Miss Mississippi. I was determined to prove Mama wrong. To prove them all wrong.

In the end, I proved her right. Second runner-up is still loser.

Close only counts in horseshoes, and it never counts at all with Mama.

16

The week before Thanksgiving I was sitting in the back booth, my customary vantage point for observing the activity at the Heartbreak Cafe. I was just thinking maybe I ought to give up my booth and go on home, because the place was busier than usual. One family of out-of-towners had been bending Dell's ear for fifteen minutes now, totally oblivious to her need to wait on other tables.

The bell over the door jingled and Purdy Overstreet came in on a waltz, twirling a skirt that was bright orange and covered with turkeys in pilgrim hats. Her hair was exactly the same color orange as the skirt, and she was wearing slinky black stockings and patent leather tap shoes that tied in the front with ribbons.

The cafe went silent—as it usually did when Purdy

showed up. She bowed and waved to her audience, and a few people laughed and applauded. Then her eyes fell on her regular booth, where the out-of-towners were still dawdling, talking about their granny in Milledgeville, Georgia, who had known Flannery O'Connor and been to the farm to feed the peacocks.

I could tell from clear across the room that Purdy didn't give a damn about Flannery or her birds; she just wanted her booth back. She glared at the strangers and stood there tapping her foot on the floor, a clicking sound that resonated throughout the room like the tick-tick-tick of a bomb about to detonate.

I was just getting to my feet to let Purdy have my booth when Hoot Everett saw his chance and took it. He raced through the crowd, bowed in front of Purdy, and invited her to join him. It was no secret, of course, that Purdy had eyes only for Scratch, but since Scratch was otherwise occupied in the kitchen, she accepted Hoot's invitation as an acceptable second choice, and Hoot led her in triumph to his table.

"There's a couple of characters for you," I said when Dell came around with coffee. I motioned toward the two lovebirds.

"About time," she said. "I thought she'd never give up on Scratch."

"Maybe Hoot's got something Scratch doesn't." I pointed to Hoot, who was handing a bottle across the table to Purdy.

Just then the door opened to admit Marvin Beckstrom, who held the lease to the Heartbreak Cafe, followed by his ubiquitous guard dog, the sheriff in full uniform, complete with pistol and handcuffs.

"Oh, Lord," Dell said. "We gotta do something fast. I don't have a liquor license, and if that bottle contains what I think it does, the sheriff could shut me down in a heartbeat. There's nothing that little turd Beckstrom would like better."

"Go," I said. "I'll distract them."

Dell headed off toward Hoot's booth, and I slid out of my seat, swiping all the dishes off onto the floor and pretending to slip and fall. It was a pretty good performance, if I say so myself. Marvin Beckstrom and the sheriff came rushing over, while Dell intercepted Hoot and Purdy and tried to wrest the bottle from them.

The sheriff lifted me to my feet, and Marvin proceeded to give me a lecture on how I should sue Dell and the Heartbreak Cafe for negligence, since it was obviously Dell's fault that I slipped. Scratch came out and started cleaning up the broken china. Across the room, the noise had escalated. Hoot was shouting, "You give that back! It ain't yours!"

Marvin and the sheriff both turned. Hoot was grabbing Purdy by the arm, and both of them looked pretty far gone. Purdy wobbled and weaved and then, as if in slow motion, went down howling.

Everybody made a beeline for her. Scratch got there

first and began to palpate Purdy's twisted leg from ankle to knee joint.

"Is it broken?" Dell asked.

"I don't think so," he said. "It's probably just a sprain. But at her age you can't be too careful. Better get her to the hospital."

I called 911, and in a couple of minutes the ambulance showed up, along with a gathering crowd of onlookers. Folks in Chulahatchie have entirely too much leisure time on their hands, if you ask me.

Purdy went into the ambulance. Hoot, determined to go with her, tried to fight the paramedics when they refused.

"I'll take him," I said. I ushered Hoot into my little blue Honda, and we took off following the ambulance the half mile to the hospital. Hoot sank into the passenger's seat and let out a sigh that filled the whole car with the odor of fermentation.

"What'd you have in that bottle, anyway?" I asked him.

"Mushcadine wine," he said. "Made it m'self. Good shtuff."

"I'll bet."

He turned in my direction and winked. "When you ain't got looks or brains, you use what you got. Better'n Viagra, my mushcadine wine."

Purdy, as it turned out, only had a sprain, but because of her age and frailty, the doctor put her in a walking cast and told her she had to have someone with her at all times.

"She lives at St. Agnes Nursing Home," I told him. "She'll be fine there. I'll take her home and get her settled."

"She ain't goin'," Hoot interrupted. "I got a spare room, and I'll take care of her. She's goin' home with me."

Purdy looked from Hoot to the doctor and back again. Then she fixed on me. "You tell Dell I want lunch brought in every day," she said. It wasn't a request; it was a command.

"Yes, ma'am."

"And I don't want Dell coming, either. *He* can bring it to me."

By *he*, I presumed her to mean Scratch. Hoot didn't like this development one bit, but he kept his mouth shut.

"Baked chicken and creamed corn casserole," she said. "Corn bread. Some of that apple pie, too." She narrowed her eyes. "You gettin' this?"

I tried to stifle a grin. "Yes, ma'am."

Must have been the smile that did it. She fixed her gaze on my face for a full two minutes, then shook a knotted, gnarled finger in my face. "You're that beauty queen— Soybean something or other. Long time ago, but I remember. You were blonde and skinny back then."

"Yes, ma'am. I'm Peach Rondell."

"Peach," she repeated. "No, that ain't right."

"Priscilla," I said. "Priscilla is my given name."

"Stupid," she muttered. "That mama of yours oughta

have known better." She gripped my hand with an arthritic claw. "You keep on being Peach, honey. It suits you."

I loaded the two of them and the collapsible wheelchair into my Honda with considerable difficulty and drove the few blocks to Hoot's house. Much to my surprise, the place was clean and neat, if a bit musty smelling. We installed Purdy in the spare room and hauled in Hoot's recliner so he'd be able to sit with her.

I went out onto the porch and called Jane Lee Custer at St. Agnes. When I'd filled her in on Purdy's condition and the fact that she was determined to let Hoot play nurse-maid, Jane Lee let out a long-suffering sigh. I could practically see her rolling her eyes.

"I presume she's done this kind of thing before," I said.

"Lord, yes," Jane Lee said. "But we can't stop her. I'll send somebody over there with clothes and her medications, and we'll check on her every day."

"She wants Dell to bring her meals from the cafe." This wasn't exactly accurate, but I figured there was no point in dragging Scratch into the picture if I could keep from it.

"All right," Jane Lee said. "Thanks for taking care of her." She paused. "Did you say you were—?"

"Yeah. Peach Rondell. I used to live here."

"We went to school together, didn't we?"

"Yes, we did." The truth was, Jane Lee Custer had been perfectly horrible to me during high school. She was destined to be a world-class brain surgeon and I was, in her words, nothing more than a breathing Barbie doll. I didn't think it would be particularly productive to remind her of that, however, especially in light of the fact that the brain surgeon thing obviously hadn't panned out so well.

"We ought to get together for lunch sometime," she said.

"Yes, let's do that."

And with both of us knowing it would never happen, not even if hell froze over, I hung up and dialed the number for the Heartbreak Cafe.

· 17 ·

The next few days made me believe—for the first time in months—that life just might be worth living. Overnight I went from observing to belonging.

Everyone wanted to hear the story of Hoot and Purdy and what happened at the emergency room. Dell and I planned Purdy's menus, and Scratch and I had a long talk about Alzheimer's and how dementia of any kind removed the filters that kept us from saying outrageous or offensive things to other people. Scratch spoke of her with such compassion and understanding that I went away revising my fictional characterization of him as an artist and painted him instead as a doctor or a counselor. Whatever he had been in his other life, he was more intelligent and more tender than any fry cook or busboy I had ever known.

At lunchtime I took Scratch to Hoot's house to deliver Purdy's meal—baked chicken, creamed corn casserole, and corn bread, just as she had ordered. Enough for two, plus half an apple-cranberry pie fresh out of the oven.

"You take direction real good," she said when she peered under the aluminum foil covers. It was her way of thanking me; Hoot's way was to slip me a pint of muscadine wine when he thought Scratch wasn't looking.

In the afternoon Boone came in and sat with me for a long time, catching me up on everything he had done since high school. It wasn't much, if truth be told—he had lived in Chulahatchie all his life except for the time he went to Ole Miss to get his master's degree in library science. I felt a little sad for him; although he had a good job and good friends, he nevertheless seemed to labor under a kind of cosmic loneliness, as if he were a visitor to an alien planet, accepted by the natives but still the only one of his species.

Some people think a family is the collection of people you're tied to by DNA. "Blood is thicker than water. Blood will tell. Ties of blood are the strongest of them all."

But that's not what being family means. Families are not the people who have to take you in, the way Mama reluctantly opened her door to me when I came back to Chulahatchie again. Families are the folks who make you feel good about yourself, who accept you as you are, who don't expect you to be perfect, who listen when you talk and let you change your mind if you need to.

Boone talked about Dell, and Dell's best friend Toni, and Scratch, and even Hoot and Purdy—as family. "Family of choice," he called them. The people you get to pick for yourself. The people whose presence makes your life deeper and richer and more fulfilling.

Sad, isn't it, that so often the people who ought to love us best, love us worst?

They don't mean to, I guess. But it's easy to take so-called real family for granted. Husbands and wives, children and parents, partners and lovers grow so familiar that they become part of the furniture of your life. You hardly think about them anymore. When you're mad or sad or scared, you take it out on them because they're there and always will be. The way you'd kick a table leg or throw a coffee cup against the wall.

God help me, I wonder if I did that with Robert— just became so accustomed to having him around that I didn't really think about how he felt or what he wanted out of life. And all of a sudden here I am with people who until a few months ago were strangers, and now they feel more like family to me than my own husband. . . .

Or my own mother.

I stopped writing and looked down. The words on the page swam as if they were underwater, blurred by unexpected tears. That old white-haired fool of a therapist delighted in such moments, when an unanticipated epiphany would rise up and slap the living daylights out of me. Pain, he was fond of saying, was progress.

Maybe he was right. But I came away with my heart stinging from the blow, all the same.

My own mother. . . .

I stared at the words again, as if they were in a language I couldn't comprehend. I waited, hoping they might sink into the page and vanish. It wasn't the first time I wished I wrote my journal in pencil, so I could just erase unwelcome insights and pretend they never happened. But of course that's not the way with therapy. You take the insights as they come and learn to recognize the important ones and follow them where they lead.

I skipped a few lines and started over:

Okay, I don't suppose I can escape it, so I might as well face it. The primal wound, the core issue. Mother.

I'm forty-five years old. Is it possible—even conceivable—that this is the first time in almost half a century I've considered whether my mother might have unfulfilled dreams, or fears I've never imagined, or pain I don't see? Is it possible—even conceivable—

that there might be a *reason* she treats me as she does, a reason beyond sheer meanness, beyond her basic disappointment in the person I turned out to be?

I need to remind myself, since the old fool isn't here to do it for me, that a reason is not an excuse. I don't have to excuse my mother for treating me the way she has all these years, even if I come to the place of understanding it. I don't even have to forgive her.

If I'm going to be honest (and why shouldn't I?—no one else is going to read this), something in me doesn't want to forgive or even to understand it. If I understand it, I might have to change my perspective, let go of the anger I've held on to all these years, abandon my image of myself as the maligned daughter, suffering under the injustice of her mother's mistreatment.

Yikes. When I put it that way, it sounds distinctly unattractive. It sounds as if I get some kind of perverse pleasure out of being misunderstood. I sound like a spoiled, selfish child who stamps her foot and throws a tantrum and in the same moment demands that she be taken seriously as a grown-up.

I don't like the direction this is going, and yet I have to follow. That's one of the rules. No erasing, no blotting out of unwelcome thoughts, no abandonment of the path when the brambles get thick and begin to draw blood.

So. If I don't like the image of myself as a spoiled brat, maybe it's time for me to act like an adult. To view my mother from the perspective of an equal, a peer, rather than a shrunk-down five-year-old. To find a way to dig past the control and manipulation and criticism and get down to the person she really is on the inside.

Suddenly I'm scared. My gut is twisting, the way it used to when I had to get onstage and perform. Maybe I don't want to be that honest with her, to put myself out there and take the risk of getting hurt again. Maybe I don't want to hear what she would say if she decided to be honest with me.

Maybe instead I'll run away and join the circus. Shoveling elephant crap isn't the worst career move in the world. Sometimes it beats the heck out of being a daughter.

Or maybe it's the same job, different title.

· 18 ·

The day before Thanksgiving I didn't go to the Heartbreak Cafe, even though it was the place I most wanted to be. Instead I stayed home and helped Tildy make pies and corn bread dressing and sweet potato soufflé.

Mama insisted on having Thanksgiving at Belladonna. We could have gone to the country club and let somebody else have the work and the mess, but she wouldn't hear of it. She was going to "do it herself," which meant that Tildy did most of the work, with me as her assistant. Mama just put the turkey in the oven and let it cook while we watched the Macy's parade on television.

When the fake Santa Claus had come and gone and the news anchors were winding up their recap, I went upstairs to take a shower. For Mama's sake, I dressed up—or as "up" as I could, considering that most of my belongings were in storage. I put on a nice pair of black slacks and a purple sequined sweater I had bought at the Near'bout New consignment shop. Mama'd have a cow if she found out I was buying secondhand clothes, but she'd also never set foot in such a place, so I figured what she didn't know wouldn't kill her.

"Nice sweater," Mama said after a cursory glance. "Gladdie Dalrymple's daughter used to have one exactly like that. You remember Gladdie, from the country club."

She turned back to the task of wrestling the turkey out of the roaster onto a serving platter. An enormous tom turkey, twenty pounds or more. Big enough for a minor Latin American country, plus two weeks' worth of leftovers.

Who did she think was going to eat all that? Daddy was gone. Melanie and Harry wouldn't think of darkening Mama's doorstep for any reason short of a funeral. It was just me and Mama.

Me and Mama and—apparently—Big Tom.

They say that recollection is most strongly tied to the sense of smell, that certain scents can raise long-buried memories to the surface. My mind flashed to Thanksgivings of my childhood—Daddy in the kitchen with a frilly bibbed apron over his white shirt, hefting the turkey onto its platter, carving with finesse and flourish, humming the old hymn "Come, Ye Thankful People, Come" under his breath.

Tears stung my eyes. What must Mama be feeling as

she set out a Thanksgiving feast for a family that would never again sit at her table? Surely somewhere deep inside she had regrets, knew she could have done better, knew she had pushed us all away with her criticism, her perfectionism, her absolute insistence on being right. But no matter what kind of stoic facade she maintained, she still had to be in pain. She had to miss Daddy more than I missed him, more than I could even imagine missing him. She had to miss her absent children.

I came up behind her. "Here, let me help," I said.

She turned and let go of the bird. It dropped with a splat back into the roaster and slung turkey drippings all over me—hair, face, and chest. I looked down to see a gob of fat lodged in the sequins and dripping down my front.

So much for dressing up.

"Look at you!" Mama said. She, of course, was still pristine and perfect, her starched white apron spotless, not a hair out of place.

I picked a bit of skin off my sleeve and popped it into my mouth. "Mmmm. Good. I think it's done."

Mama gaped at me for a full thirty seconds, and we both started to laugh. I laughed so hard I cried, and then I laughed so hard I peed—not much, just a little leak, but enough that I had to change the pants as well as the sweater.

Lord, I don't ever remember laughing like that with my mother. Never.

"Tell you what," I said when we'd both regained our

composure. "I'll put the turkey on the platter and slice it, and *then* I'll go change clothes. Can you handle the gravy?"

Mama gave me a disdainful look. "I've been making gravy since before you were born," she said.

And always lumpy, I thought. But I didn't say so. No point in ruining a tender moment with the truth.

In all the years I lived at home, Thanksgiving at Belladonna was never like Thanksgiving at anyone else's house. While other folks were having second helpings of pie and cheering their team to victory, or sleeping off their excesses, or gathering on the porch swing to escape the heat of the kitchen, at Mama's house we were all working.

Thanksgiving Day was the day the Christmas decorations went up, and in a house as big as Belladonna, that meant a bloody blue million lights. Lights inside, in every room, on every mantelpiece. Lights outside in every bush and tree. A fairyland of lights—white ones outside, multicolored ones inside. Tasteful, tiny lights, thousands of them. Greenery everywhere. Two enormous trees, one in the front parlor and one in the den. Mama's house at Christmas was like a spread out of *Southern Living.*

I hadn't done it for years, of course, but I remembered, and I was dreading it. Not just the actual hard work of decorating, but the ache of doing it without Daddy.

About halfway through the turkey and dressing, however, Mama set down her fork and gave me the look that meant I'd better come to attention. "I've made a decision," she said.

I held my breath.

"It just doesn't seem reasonable to put up all those decorations this year." She shrugged, as if this was a casual statement, but the sidelong glance told me it was freighted with a significance she didn't want to admit. "I thought maybe we could just do the tree in the front parlor and then electric candles in the windows. Understated. Elegant."

"Less is more?" I said.

"Exactly." Mama looked at me with relief. "You're not disappointed?"

"Lord, no, I'm relieved," I blurted out.

Mama narrowed her eyes.

"Well, you know," I hedged, "with Daddy not here—"

"Yes," she said, too brightly. "Your father always loved Christmas at Belladonna, all the lights and decorations. The people. The parties."

One of my mother's innate gifts was her ability to mold the truth to suit herself. In reality, Daddy hated the way Mama made Christmas into such an extravaganza, hated the constant coming and going of the country club crowd, hated the open houses and the late nights and the frenetic activity of getting ready beforehand and cleaning up after. He would have loved a quiet Christmas with family and a few friends, a yule log in the fireplace, hot chocolate or hot toddies, stories around the tree.

Daddy was Norman Rockwell. Mama was Neiman Marcus.

She picked at a slice of turkey and made circles in the gravy with the tines of her fork.

"Mama," I said, "how are you doing with Daddy gone?"

"I'm fine," she said, but to me her voice didn't sound normal.

It was the briefest of glimpses at the real Donna Rondell, the human one, the one who wasn't perfectly in control every moment of every day. She turned away from me, but I caught it nevertheless—the tears welling up in her eyes, the lump in her throat she couldn't quite swallow down.

She hadn't cried the day of the funeral. She'd been too busy marshaling the troops—making sure my sister set up the reception room just right, making sure my brother had on the right suit and tie for the occasion. Never mind that Melanie was fifty-something and quite capable of centering a vase of flowers. Never mind that Harry had been dressing himself for more than forty years. Never mind that all of us were devastated by the suddenness of Daddy's death. Diagnosed with leukemia, dead in ten days. We hadn't even had a chance to get there to say good-bye.

The week of the funeral was the last straw for both Harry and Melanie. For years Harry had been—in the words of my therapist—emotionally absent and disconnected from the rest of the family. He always had a way of letting Mama's criticisms roll off him like water off a duck. I envied his ability to remain unaffected by her nagging, even though it meant he was shut off from all of us. He simply refused to engage, and that disengagement meant that none of us ever saw beyond the surface image that Harry wanted to present. Maybe Daddy knew more than the rest of us, but if so, any understanding of the inner Harry died with him.

I tried to talk to my brother once, about the way Mama's expectations made me feel about myself. His answer was, "Don't let it bother you." That was Harry's answer to everything. He just abdicated from the family and went his own way.

Melanie, on the other hand, had always been far *too* engaged with Mama, too intent on trying to please, to be the perfect daughter. She catered to Mama, but she adored Daddy, and when he died, something in her snapped. "She doesn't *care*," she said to me at the visitation. "Look at her; she hasn't shed a single tear."

Melanie held herself together through the formalities of death, and then she shattered into a thousand pieces. Mama never said a word to me about my sister's nervous breakdown or admitted that she had been hospitalized. If my mother didn't acknowledge something, it didn't exist. Such things didn't happen to "our kind of people."

The week of Daddy's funeral was the last time Melanie had set foot in Chulahatchie and, to my knowledge, the last time she had spoken to Mama.

"It's okay, Mama," I said now. "It's okay to miss him. It's okay to cry."

"I'm not crying. I just think—well, since it will only be the two of us here, there's no point in making a big production of decorating, is there?"

"You know, Mama, if you want to talk about . . . things—"

She jumped on this like white on rice. "What kind of things?"

"I don't know, just things. How you've been since Daddy's gone. What's going on in your mind and"—I hesitated—"in your heart."

Blurted out like that, it didn't sound open or compassionate, just stupid. I should have thought this through more. Maybe I'd underestimated that old fool of a therapist. Maybe he knew more about what he was doing than I gave him credit for.

I tried again. "You've never talked to me about Daddy's death."

"You haven't talked to me about what happened with Robert," she countered.

She was right. I hadn't. I'd told Dell Haley and Boone Atkins more about the breakup of my marriage than I'd told my own mother. But then, I had more reason to expect Dell and Boone to be understanding and supportive.

Still, pain is progress. I had to try.

"I don't know how to explain it. We had my birthday dinner—a nice, romantic evening with friends. Then the next thing I knew, he left a voice-mail message informing me he had met someone else and was leaving." I pulled in a ragged breath and tried to suppress the waves of emotion that were threatening to surface. "A *voice mail*! He didn't even have the guts to tell me face-to-face."

"What did you do?" Mama asked.

"I didn't know what to do. I was in shock. I—"

She waved a hand in a dismissive gesture. "No, I mean, what did you do that would make him up and leave like that?"

Of course she would think I was to blame. I must be at fault—I had never done anything in my life that earned the Donna Rondell seal of approval. I stared at her, flabbergasted, while Intermittent Hope cackled its evil, mocking laughter in the back of my mind.

People who wax nostalgic and write songs about being "home for the holidays" never had a home like Belladonna or a holiday like one with Mama. Thanksgiving dinner took most of two days to prepare; eating it took about seventeen and a half minutes, not counting dessert and coffee.

By the time I finished putting the food away and hand-washing the crystal and china, Mama had dragged decorations from the upstairs closet, arranged electric candles in all the windows, lined the parlor mantel with greenery and lights, and strung white icicle lights around the perimeter of the front porch railing.

This was Mama's idea of a minimal Christmas.

"We'll have to leave the rest until Monday," she said, waving a hand vaguely in the direction of the corner where a settee had been moved to make way for the Christmas tree. The tree itself had already been delivered and was sitting in a bucket of water behind the carriage house. Tildy's nephew Glover had been conscripted to come on Monday morning to bring it into the house and set it up.

Glover played defensive end for the Alabama Crimson Tide, and he could probably bench-press the eight-foot fir tree, including the cast-iron base, with one hand. He was a sweet-natured, tenderhearted boy who smiled incessantly and hummed hymn tunes under his breath. Tomorrow he'd be facing an intimidating front line, crushing heads and snapping bones and grinning and humming the whole time.

Neither Mama nor I much liked football, but we promised Tildy we'd watch the game on TV. Glover was supposed to wave to us from the sidelines.

"That's it for now, I suppose," Mama said, sounding almost wistful at the prospect of having no more work to do.

"It's a pretty day," I said. "I think I'll go for a walk."

Before she could stop me or find something else that needed doing, I dashed upstairs, grabbed my journal, and flew out the front door, letting the screen slam behind me.

The afternoon was warmish and sun-streaked, the streets of Chulahatchie uncommonly quiet. Here and there I heard a dog bark, or the sounds of cheering through an open screen door as the afternoon football game progressed. On the blacktop in the schoolyard, a couple of teenagers were playing one-on-one, and a little girl was riding a pink bicycle in a circle around the outside of the court.

"Don't get off the sidewalk," one of the boys said, and the girl nodded. Big brother taking care of little sister, I surmised.

Quite apart from conscious awareness, my steps took me past the schoolyard, past the square, all the way down East Main to Cypress Street and the wide, rolling lawns of the cemetery.

There it was, up on a hill just to the left of the big mausoleum and the cypress circle. Daddy's plot.

I labored up the steep hill, feeling the strain in my calves, and came at last to the stone that said RONDELL in bold Gothic capitals. On one side, Daddy's name and dates were engraved, and below, in script, words I had chosen against Mama's will: *The world is poorer without you.*

It was a fluke, really. Mama had ordered *Loving Husband and Father,* or some such meaningless tripe. I happened to answer the telephone when the engraver called to confirm the spelling of Daddy's name, and I made the change without Mama ever knowing it.

I wondered if she noticed. Wondered if she ever came out here to sit, to talk to Daddy, to mourn. I had no idea. Perhaps I'd never know.

On the right was Mama's name and birthdate, with the date of death left blank. I wondered idly what would be engraved on her side. *The world is richer without you?*

More peaceful, anyway.

I leaned against the shoulder of the headstone, above Mama's name, and tested it to see if it would hold my weight. It didn't move, so I propped my butt up on it and sat down. If I was going to be sacrilegious, or at the very least disrespectful, I figured I oughta do it on Mama's side.

"Well, Daddy," I said, "I'm home. You always kept asking me why I didn't come and telling me how much Mama missed me. I'm pretty sure you were the one who missed me, and not her. I missed you, too. But I expect you understand it more now, at least if what we were taught in Sunday school is even halfway true."

I paused and listened to the faint music of wind in the branches of the cypress trees. Why, I wondered, did people traditionally plant cypress trees in graveyards? Was it because they were evergreen and symbolic of eternal life? Or because they loomed like terrifying creatures of the night, waiting for the right moment to pick up their roots and walk?

With some effort I dragged my eyes from the bowing cypress branches and fixed my attention on my father's tombstone. "Being back in Chulahatchie is strange," I said. "I don't belong here, and yet . . ."

I let the sentence slide, the thought unfinished. *And yet what?*

And yet I don't belong with Robert anymore, either.

I don't belong . . . anywhere. With anyone.

It wasn't entirely true; I knew it even as the words formed themselves inside my skull. I had friends here, or at least the beginnings of friendships. I had Boone and Dell and all the folks at the Heartbreak Cafe.

But I couldn't get past the rejections: Charles Chase, Robert, my own mother.

"What did I do wrong?" I whispered—to my daddy, to the wind, to the cypress trees. To God or fate or anyone who might listen and answer.

No response, not even from the wind in the branches.

I said it again, louder: "What did I do wrong?"

And from behind me, a quiet voice replied, "Maybe nothing."

I jerked around. There stood Boone Atkins, not six feet behind me.

"Dang, Boone!" I said. "I thought you were God."

He chuckled. "No one's ever made that mistake before."

"Well, okay, not God, exactly. But still, you scared the bejesus out of me." I paused. "Or into me."

A light came on in his eyes, and he laughed out loud this time. "Peach, I was raised Catholic. We have a history of trying to frighten people into faith, and trust me, it doesn't work very well."

"What are you doing here on Thanksgiving afternoon?" I asked.

"Visiting." He pointed down the way, toward the family plot I had passed on my way up the hill. "Mother died on November twenty-sixth," he said. "I come every year."

"I'm sorry." The words of consolation sounded hollow and empty, but I didn't know what else to say.

"Me, too." He settled himself on the chilly grass and nodded in the direction of Daddy's headstone. "You getting any answers?"

"Not really." I turned to him. "God, Boone, my life has been so awful the past year. The thing with Robert came totally out of the blue, and I didn't know how to handle it. Then I came home—a huge mistake, but what other choice did I have? And then . . . well, you know. Another major blunder. It feels as if the universe is conspiring against me. Like I've got really, really bad karma. I repeat my question: *What did I do wrong?*"

"And I repeat my answer: *Maybe nothing.*"

I stared at him. "What do you mean?"

"You seem to believe that you get back only what you put into life."

"Well, yes, don't you? Isn't it a principle, you reap what you sow?"

"Technically," he said. "But I think you're missing the bigger picture. Just because life is difficult right now doesn't necessarily mean you've done something horrible to deserve it. Maybe life moves in cycles—like the seasons, like the tides. Winter comes because it comes. And spring comes, too—maybe not as quickly as we'd like it to, but always right on time."

"You're saying everything happens for a reason."

"No. Some things just happen. Take your relationship with Robert, for example. Maybe there were signs you could have seen, but even if you'd seen them, could you have prevented the ultimate outcome? If he was determined to move on, nothing you could have done would have stopped him. We don't know the reasons things happen, and even if we did, we can't necessarily change the rhythms of life. What we can do is find grace in the change, and find joy in the grace."

He got to his feet and laid a hand on my shoulder. "Don't fight it so much," he said. "Breathe. Float with the current for a while. Give yourself a break. You'll figure it out in the end."

That night, after Mama went to bed, I took the phone, went out onto the back verandah, and called Melanie.

"Can you believe it?" I said. "She lured me into talking about the breakup with Robert, and then she turned around and blamed me!"

"What do you expect?" she said. "You know how she is."

"I know. I just thought—"

"You just thought this time it would be different." Melanie sounded curt and irritable. "But it's not different, and it will never be different. This is our mother we're talking about."

I felt something writhing in my gut—something old and familiar, like the memory of some cataclysm from childhood that my adult mind had blocked out but my body remembered.

"She keeps putting up walls, Mel. I can't get through to her."

"Well, if you can't, nobody can," Melanie said. "You were always her favorite. Nobody else ever existed."

The earth lurched, and I almost fell out of my chair. *I* was Mama's favorite? No. That was Melanie's role. Ladylike Melanie. Perfect Melanie. "What are you talking about?" I said. "My whole life I was held up to the standard you set—and I always came up lacking."

"Are you kidding?" she said. "You were Miss Ole Miss. First runner-up to Miss Mississippi."

"Second runner-up," I corrected. "And she's never let me forget it."

"Listen to me," Melanie said. "You will never please that woman. Never. You will never live up to her standards of perfection. And if you try, you'll drive yourself right into a nervous breakdown. Trust me. I know."

The way she said those four words made my blood run cold. *Trust me. I know.*

"I know you do," I whispered, half hoping she wouldn't hear. "You've been there."

A long, long silence stretched between us—me in Chulahatchie, Melanie in California, as far away as she could get without dropping off the edge of the continent.

"Happy Thanksgiving, kiddo," she said. "Take care of yourself."

And then she was gone.

· 19 ·

A week isn't a very long time unless you're waiting for something to happen, and then it feels like forever.

Dell had closed the Heartbreak Cafe and gone off somewhere, so I didn't have any place to get away to and ended up being stuck in the house with Mama. For a solid week I kept to my room (with breaks now and then for leftover turkey and dressing and pumpkin pie, when Mama wasn't around to criticize). I sat at my desk, journaling. I sat at the window, staring.

Pacing. Writing. Thinking. Trying not to think.

I couldn't get out of my mind what Mama had said about the meltdown of my marriage. The implication that I was at fault, somehow. That I had done something heinous to bring it on myself.

It's all in my journal—the pain, the self-loathing, the shame and blame. What could I have done differently to make him love me? How could I have changed, reinvented myself, become the person he wanted me to be? How could I, at forty-five, become younger, sexier, more attractive, more . . . interesting?

And the other side of the seesaw, the pure white rage and indignation. How dare he leave me? How could he have done it—been so fickle and shortsighted and downright stupid to think that his life would be better without me, when I had been the good and faithful wife all these years?

Reality, of course, lay somewhere in between, in that grainy marital netherworld, the bleak and colorless space where the words *We grew apart* had meaning beyond some limping, lame excuse.

At last, I wrote myself into a modicum of balance and reason:

In truth, I do not believe that Robert is an evil person or that he deliberately set out to hurt me.

What I do believe is that he is the kind of man who needs constant affirmation, and the bottom line is, I knew him too well. There comes a point in any marriage where you're no longer awed by your spouse's impressive intellect or willing to worship at the shrine of his superiority. And Robert always needed to be venerated. Needed someone to polish his pedestal and gaze lovingly up at him and turn a blind eye to his humanity.

On the other hand, I expect I was pretty dull company. Most of the jobs I held over the course of our marriage were low-risk secretarial or administrative positions, not at all what I envisioned as a career when I was in college. Not interesting enough to talk about over dinner and certainly no competition for profound philosophies.

I never shared with Robert my desire to write or attempted to follow that dream. For one thing, he held the role of designated thinker, designated writer, designated idea person. Publishing obtuse articles in obscure philosophical journals made him the expert— and something of a literary snob. He never had patience for what he called (with a curl of the lip) "commercial writing"—which was anything, fiction or nonfiction, that brought in a living wage or could be understood by a moderately educated person.

Besides that, he didn't want me to have dreams— or to do much of anything except facilitate his climb up the academic ladder. By the time he made chair of the philosophy department, he was ready for me to quit working. He wanted me to be available at a moment's notice to pull together a faculty dinner or host his grad students, who ate us out of house and home and sat up until midnight and beyond drinking cheap wine and discussing incomprehensible philosophical constructs.

Now Robert is well on his way to provost and, eventually, perhaps even chancellor. He needs, if not a trophy wife, at least a spouse who adores him, and whose claim to fame lies in accomplishments more erudite than being Miss Ole Miss and second runner-up to Miss Mississippi.

When I look back on my life with Robert, I can't help but wonder: How much of myself did I abandon to his ambitions? How much of my soul did I abdicate? I didn't care about university politics. He didn't care about anything else.

I've thought a lot about what Boone said to me— how life has its rhythms, like the seasons or the tides, and although we can't control the changes, we can find the grace and the joy.

I think at last I know what the grace is.

I'm holding it in my hands.

When the phone finally rang on Sunday afternoon, my heart leaped to hear Boone Atkins's voice on the other end.

And then it sank.

"Robbed?" I yelled into the receiver, and Boone's voice came back to me, soft, shaken. Yes, Dell's cafe had been broken into and robbed. And Scratch—dear, sweet, gentle, compassionate Scratch—was accused of the crime.

I left without telling Mama where I was going and got to the Heartbreak Cafe just as Boone and Toni arrived.

"What happened?"

Boone pointed toward the front door, which hung crazily from one hinge. "You know as much as we do. Come on."

Toni was already inside, clutching Dell in a bone-crushing hug. I wondered if I was the only one who noticed Dell wasn't hugging back. *What is going on between the two of them?* I wondered. But I didn't have time to find out.

Dell sat down and put her face in her hands. "Whoever did it took everything in the cash register and maybe last week's till as well. Sheriff is dead set that Scratch did it. They're out looking for him right now."

I looked from her to Toni and back again. "Then we need to find him first."

"The sheriff hasn't found him yet," Dell said. "What makes you think we can?"

"I don't know, but we have to try." I hauled Boone up by one hand. "Come on."

I hustled Boone out the door and thrust the keys into his hand. "You drive," I said. "I need to think."

We circled around the courthouse and headed out of town toward the river, driving aimlessly, watching the side roads. "Where are we going?" Boone asked.

"I don't know. We just needed to get out of the cafe and give Dell and Toni some privacy."

He shot me a confused look. "What do you mean?"

"It's obvious something is going on between those two, and they need to talk about it."

"How on earth could you possibly know that?"

I shrugged. "I watch people. I pay attention."

"If you decide to do something besides being a writer, try psychology," he said. "You'd be really good at it."

I laughed, but it came out more like a sarcastic bark. "Right. All those dysfunctional relationships in my life might disagree with you."

"We've all got skeletons," he said, "and we've all got baggage. But you've got a lot of insight. You'll come out just fine."

"Before I'm dead, I hope. And in the meantime just think how much material I'll have for the Great American Novel."

Boone was silent for several minutes, and when he spoke again, his voice held a touch of nostalgia. "You know, I remember when we were friends all those years ago," he said. "Your mother didn't like me much, as I recall. My family wasn't in the same league as yours—you know, country club, Jaycees, all that."

"Yeah," I said. "All that."

He chuckled. "When we get older, we begin to realize how foolish such distinctions can be. How they separate us from people who truly might be our soul mates."

"Mama's seventy-nine years old, and she has yet to learn that lesson," I said. "Besides, it's hard to know your soul mates if you don't recognize your own soul."

"You remember that dance, when I took you home after your date got his nose broken?"

I smiled at him. "It was his jaw, actually. Poor Robbie. He was no match for Marshall Threadgood."

"Actually, as it turns out, they were a pretty good match," Boone said. "They've been together for almost twenty years."

"You mean, like, business partners?"

"I mean, like, *life partners*," Boone said. "Yep. Marsh and Robbie. They live in Tuscaloosa. Robbie's a tenured professor at Alabama, teaching medieval history. Marsh is assistant football coach at one of the high schools."

I felt my jaw drop. "You're kidding."

"Nope. Cross my heart." Boone grinned over at me. "I have dinner with them every now and then," he said. "Marsh went over to the W and took some classes at its culinary school. He's quite a good chef."

He made a right turn onto a gravel road. "I don't know how long you're staying in Chulahatchie, but maybe you could go with me sometime."

"I'd like that."

I turned and gazed out the window. It was early December; the trees were bare, and where underbrush would flourish knee-high in the spring and summer, the ground was now thickly padded with leaves and pine needles. Still, there was something familiar about this road.

"Where are we going?" I asked.

"I had a thought," Boone said. "An idea of where

Scratch might have gone. Probably a wild-goose chase, but—"

The road curved, and, despite how different the woods looked, the house was still there, still the same. A box on stilts, with a wide screened porch facing the river and a walkway leading down to a dock over the brown waters of the Tennessee-Tombigbee.

Charles Chase's river camp.

Coincidence. It had to be. I held my breath and averted my eyes, waiting for us to pass by.

But Boone was pulling into the driveway. At the front of the cabin sat the sheriff's car with lights flashing.

"What are we doing here?" I said. I hoped he wouldn't answer, hoped I wouldn't have to hear a truth I didn't want to face.

"This is Dell's place," Boone said absentmindedly.

He wasn't paying attention to me. Instead, he was watching the drama playing out down on the dock. Like a silent film, the scene spun out: the sheriff striding down the planks with his hand on the butt of his pistol; Scratch getting up and facing him; the handcuffs, the long walk back to the car . . .

"What do you mean, Dell's place?" I said.

He frowned. "Well, it's a fishing camp. Belonged to Dell's husband, Chase, before he died. Now it's hers. But it hasn't been used in months."

"How'd you know Scratch would be here?"

"Lucky guess."

He got out of the car and walked toward Scratch and the sheriff. I could see him gesturing, arguing, but I couldn't bring myself to watch. All I could see, on the screen in the back of my mind, was an image of myself climbing those stairs, or sitting on the end of that dock in the moonlight or—

I opened the car door, ran for the trees, and retched into the leaves at the edge of the woods.

No one noticed.

· 20 ·

I didn't have any choice but to go back to the cafe with Boone. To do otherwise would have raised far too many questions, questions I didn't even want to consider myself, much less have to answer for anyone else.

My years on the pageant circuit had taught me how to smile when I wanted to cry, to interact when I wanted to scream, and above all, to keep a tight rein on my emotions and not let them interfere with business at hand. That afternoon I gave the performance of a lifetime.

Not that anyone would have known any difference. They were all too focused on Scratch, on his arrest.

Something had happened in the time we'd been gone. Dell and Toni had reconciled and were best friends again. Writer's curiosity always prodded me toward details, and

I wondered, just briefly, what the source of their conflict might be. But the thought passed quickly, absorbed in the weightier matters of the moment.

Boone, Toni, and Dell went to the sheriff's office to try to see Scratch. I stayed at the cafe, although leaving someone there to protect things seemed a bit futile.

As soon as they were out the door, my protective wall crumbled. I cried, I paced, I walked in circles. I considered packing up my car and leaving town without a word. I wanted to be as far away from Chulahatchie as I could get—away from Dell Haley and the Heartbreak Cafe and everyone there I had ever dared to call my friend.

Finally I made a pot of coffee, settled into my booth, and opened my journal.

Can it possibly be true? Charles Chase was Dell's husband? That sweet teddy bear of a man who laughed with his entire body and juggled fruit in the produce aisle of the Piggly Wiggly? Unfaithful to Dell, with me?

I want to convince myself otherwise, say, "It can't be. It's a mistake. A dreadful, horrible mistake." But we were there. At the river camp where he and I made love. Had sex. Whatever term applies. Some very nasty metaphors come to mind.

The thought of it makes me want to throw up again.

Boone said it: "Dell's husband, Chase." I'm snagged

up on the names: Charles Chase, Chase Haley. But who else could it be?

Who else?

It was his cabin. His porch. His dock. It was the place I knew so well, the place that could spill all the intimate details about me, if the walls had eyes and ears to watch and listen, and a tongue to tell the tale.

And I believed him. *I believed him.* Believed that he was divorced, or almost so; that his wife was unreasonable and indifferent and didn't understand him. Believed all the lies. Or if I didn't believe them, I wanted to. Because I wanted to be wanted. I wanted it so much I didn't even think about who else I might be hurting, who might be devastated by his infidelity, whose soul might be scarred for all time because of my indiscretion.

Indiscretion? What kind of sappy, self-justifying word is that? It wasn't an "indiscretion." It didn't "just happen." It wasn't a "mistake"—oops, I spelled the word wrong and have to scratch it out and correct it.

There's no eraser for something like this.

For me, or for the woman I call my friend.

And what about Chase, or Charles, or whatever his name was? Mama told me that Dell's husband had died. A heart attack? I don't remember—it just went right over my head (since, of course, it didn't concern me directly).

I feel as if I'm floating above myself, seeing myself through someone else's eyes. And what I see is a self-centered, childish, over-the-hill beauty queen desperately trying to hang on to her image of herself as attractive and desirable and worthy of love and attention. I want to say, "This is not who I am," but even as I think the words, I feel myself stomping my foot and planting my hands on my hips like a spoiled five-year-old.

God, release me from this captivity.

Was that a prayer? I don't know. I'm desperate enough to pray, no matter that I haven't done it in years. But if there is a god or a goddess out there listening, some universal benevolence capable of intervening in human life (and willing to do so)—even then, what would I ask? She is no genie who can grant three wishes, and besides, I've read enough books to know you have to be very careful what you wish for.

I sat there staring at the page, its rounded corners and faint blue lines, its darker blue ink. The handwriting not neat and precise, as it usually was, but shaky and uneven, exactly the way I felt on the inside.

I had to do something. Had to change something.

And yet there was nothing that could be changed. Charles was Dell Haley's husband, and he was dead. The logical part of my mind kept telling me that I wasn't responsible for his death, and still I felt like I had killed him.

I had killed something, anyway. A friendship, certainly.

A connection. Perhaps the last faint vestige of my own self-worth.

I turned back to the page and wrote two words:

Adulterer. Murderer.

The admission did not relieve the guilt that clung to me. I was suffocating under its weight, pushed beneath the water and held there to drown.

Then I heard the bell jingle as the broken door was shoved open on its single hinge.

Dell and the others had returned.

Boone and Toni filled me in. Dell sat with her head in her hands, letting her coffee get cold while the talk swirled around her. I put on my best poker face and listened intently, and fortunately I didn't have to look Dell in the eye.

"The sheriff's just assuming Scratch did it," Toni said, "even though it doesn't make a lick of sense. Why on earth would he break down the front door when he's got keys to the place? And if he did steal the money, where is it? And why would he be still hanging around town, lolling on the dock at Chase's fishing camp, just waiting for somebody to come and arrest him?"

I flinched at the mention of the river camp but kept my eyes fixed on Toni Champion. She was older than I was, by ten years or so, but she had the kind of classic beauty that only improved with age. She reminded me of Katharine

Hepburn—long and lean and self-assured, with an elegant neck and piercing eyes. She carried herself with the grace of a wild animal, fiercely independent, ready to defend to the death those she loved. I wondered what she would do if she knew I had betrayed Dell by sleeping with Charles.

I hoped I'd never find out.

"Anyway," Boone said, picking up where Toni had left off, "we found out a lot about Scratch that nobody knew. He was married once, to a woman named Alyssa, and had a baby girl. He was premed, and his wife was prelaw."

"Scratch? A doctor?" I recalled the fictional sketches that filled my journal, my characterization of him first as a failed artist and then as a physician with a mysterious barrier to fulfilling his life's calling. Guess I wasn't too far off. And his wife, a lawyer? "Sounds like a match made in heaven," I said.

"You'd think so," Toni said. "But his father-in-law—who was also a lawyer, and a very successful, high-powered one—disapproved of the marriage."

"Disapproved so much," Boone said, "that he managed to have him arrested on charges of breaking and entering—"

"No," Toni interrupted. "Aggravated assault. A felony."

"Right," Boone said. "Five years in prison, I think. That's how the sheriff managed to hold him without evidence on the robbery charge. Said he'd violated parole and couldn't be released until the paperwork got straightened out."

I thought of Scratch in that jail cell, and the image came to mind of a sleek, muscular panther pacing back and forth in the cramped cage of a zoo. "So what happens now?" I said.

"We have to get a lawyer," Toni said.

All this time, Dell had said not a word. She still sat there staring at her coffee cup, tracing a design with one finger across the Formica tabletop.

"What did you say Scratch's full name is?" I asked.

Dell answered without looking up. "John Michael Greer."

"And his wife?"

"Alyssa, I think."

I pulled a paper napkin out of the dispenser and wrote the names down.

I couldn't do anything to help Dell or her dead husband or myself. The least I could do was try to help Scratch.

I found her—and it wasn't hard, given the information I'd gleaned. An attractive black female lawyer in Atlanta with a high-powered father? I wagered everyone would know Alyssa Greer, and I was right. All it took was one call to Lydia, my old suitemate at the W.

I met Lydia when I was eighteen and a freshman. Our sophomore year we shared a suite, and when I transferred to Ole Miss my junior year, Lydia stayed on at the W. But by the time I was a senior and about to be crowned Miss Ole Miss, she had already finished her bachelor's degree, entered law school, and was well on her way to becoming the youngest woman judge ever to sit on the Georgia State Supreme Court. From being shy as wallpaper during her first two years in college, the woman had morphed into a legal genius.

"Dang, Peach," she said when she heard my voice, "I figured you were off on tour as Miss Middle-Aged America by now."

"Very funny. You know everybody in the Georgia court system, right?"

"Pretty much," she said. "You planning to commit a felony?"

"I'm looking for someone. A lawyer, I think. Woman named Alyssa Greer."

There was a pause, a chuckle. "You really know how to pick 'em, girl."

Once I met Alyssa Greer, I understood what Lydia meant. For one thing, she was the most beautiful woman I had ever seen—and being on the pageant circuit, I had met a lot of beauties up close, personal, and nearly naked. But Alyssa had something more than physical attractiveness. She had a strength about her, a centeredness that both drew me to her and confounded me.

It took her about five minutes to do what none of us had been able to accomplish—to bully down the sheriff and get Scratch released. Their reunion in the Heartbreak Cafe was a sight to behold, one of those moments when time suspends and the love crackles like static electricity in the air. I couldn't have imagined a better scene if I had written it myself.

Oh, yes, I liked Alyssa. Liked her and respected her and wished I could be more like her. Here was a woman who had gone through some very hard times and come out stronger. A woman of deep character, who didn't let one mistake early in her life define her.

Alyssa Greer was a velvet brick.

And besides all that, she brought faith into my world.

I gravitated to the little girl the moment I saw her. "Hello," I said.

The child ducked her head, tentative as a butterfly, but she had been taught how to shake hands, and her grip was firm. Then she looked up at me with wide doe eyes, Hershey's chocolate eyes, and smiled.

I melted into a puddle and never recovered.

Her name was Imani—"Faith" in Swahili, and she was eight years old. We became best friends. We colored together, told stories, laughed, and generally kept ourselves occupied while Alyssa and Scratch were sorting out the legalities of his situation and getting to know one another again and trying to help Dell figure out who robbed the cafe.

Mama would have been scandalized—her precious daughter, her golden child, joined at the hip with a little black girl. But I was happier than I had been in ages. For the first time in years, my mind and heart were occupied with something besides myself. While I wasn't looking, joy—always elusive when I chased it—tiptoed up behind me and settled over me like a benediction.

I was happy. So happy that I almost forgot about Charles and Dell and the fishing camp and the affair and my own burning shame.

Almost.

Until Dell offered Scratch and Alyssa and Imani use of the house on the river.

I might be able to let it go, if I didn't have to think about Imani out there every blessed day.

Now I can't get it out of my mind—those rustic rooms, lit by candlelight; the image of my flabby middle-aged self and Charles Chase making utter fools of ourselves like hormonal teenagers; the fear that some evidence has been left behind, something that would tie me to the river camp and Charles and my guilt.

I don't know what to do—to confess it all and unburden my soul or to live with the guilt as punishment for my sins. I remember Charles once said that the Catholics had it partly right—that there is a purgatory, only it's in this life, not the next one. Is this my penance, to keep silent and bear the weight of a knowledge that would only hurt the people I care about?

Or is that the coward's way—to say nothing and

hope no one finds out, so that I won't have to face the look of utter outrage on Dell Haley's face?

God, what a burden it is to live with a secret that could destroy everything you value! These people are my friends, and now that I'm connected to them, they feel like a lifeline, an umbilical cord that ties me to reality and nourishes my soul. They are my family. I don't want to feel their hurt or anger or disappointment. But I also don't want to hide from them—even the parts of myself I'm ashamed of.

I'm pretty sure I know what that old fool of a therapist would tell me: You can never be certain of another person's love unless you let others see you as you really are.

But what if I let them see me, and they turn away?

In the end, Dell Haley saved me the trouble of further navel-gazing.

The third week in December, after Scratch and Alyssa and Imani had been living out at the river camp for a while, I was in my accustomed booth in the cafe, writing frantically in my journal, as if the very act of putting words on paper might save my life.

Dell came over with the coffeepot and poured me a refill. "You got a minute, Peach?"

I slammed the book shut and swallowed, hard. "Sure. Have a seat."

She sat. I waited. She had an odd, closed look on her

face, as if she'd rather be anywhere on earth than sitting across the table from me.

"Listen, Peach," she said, "I need to talk to you about something."

"Okay." I leaned forward, sure that she could hear my heart hammering in my chest. "Is anything wrong?"

"It's about—well, about your journal."

"What about it?"

"Remember the day Purdy Overstreet sprained her ankle? You left your journal in the cafe when you went to the hospital and came in to get it the next day?"

"I remember."

"Well—"

I looked into her eyes, and in that moment I knew. She had read it. She knew everything. I struggled to keep my voice calm and steady. "Did you read it?"

"I'm sorry, Peach. I shouldn't have done it."

"No, you shouldn't have. I trusted you."

"But the thing is," she went on with a great deal of effort, "there's something in there I need to know, and you're the only one who can tell me." She tried to take a sip of her coffee, but her hand shook, so she just gripped the cup and forged ahead. "You wrote about my husband, Chase, and the woman he was having an affair with. The river camp. The meeting between the two of them. Who was she, Peach? And how did you know?"

Oh, my God, I thought. *She thinks it's someone else.*

The words in my head came out of my mouth, an involuntary groan: "Oh, my God."

I couldn't have lied to her then if my neck had been in the guillotine and a single falsehood would keep the blade from flashing down. I began to cry, to sob, to weep with such force that it felt as if my soul were being ripped up out of my gut. "No," I heard someone moan. "Please, no." It was my voice wailing, my heart shattering. I thought I had known heartache before, but the loss of my relationship with Robert was nothing—*nothing*—compared with the loss of this friend who had accepted me with such grace.

"Oh, God, Dell, I'm so, so sorry."

"Sorry for what? I'm the one who needs to apologize. For violating your privacy. For reading your journal."

I stared at her. She didn't understand. She didn't *know*.

"The man," I managed to get out, "the river camp. The woman. It was me."

"It wasn't you. It was a tall, thin, blonde woman. It was—"

In a flash of insight I understood. At Boone's encouragement, I had written a few of my journal entries as fictional scenes. This one was only a few paragraphs, a brief scene in which I experimented with recasting my relationship with Charles Chase from a third-person point of view. The initial seduction, the first meeting. Not the way it happened in reality, of course, but what else is fiction good for if not for improving on the raw material of one's personal life?

Dell would never have recognized the woman I described in that journal entry. I had painted the Other Woman—me—as I used to be, maybe as I wished I still was. At the very least, the way Charles made me feel, for a moment or two: Thin. Beautiful. Desirable.

"I didn't know, Dell," I said. "I didn't know he was your husband. I didn't know he was anybody's husband. He told me he was divorced."

I saw the flash of pain across her face, as if someone had stabbed her with a blade.

"He told me his name was Charles."

Dell bit her lip. "His name *was* Charles. Chase was a nickname. No one ever called him anything else."

I mumbled some other sentences, about the river camp and discretion and how no one knew. Meaningless, all of it. None of it mattered—not the pain, not the rationalization.

The closed expression on her face, the sense of being shut and locked out. It was exactly what I deserved, of course, but still it hurt like hell. I wanted to get away, to run and never show my face inside the Heartbreak Cafe ever again. But there was one more thing that had to be done, one more truth that needed to be spoken.

"Dell," I said, "the last time I was with him, he told me he couldn't see me anymore. He told me he was married and that he had to try to make things right." I blew out a breath, trying to exhale the stress inside. "He loved you, Dell. He always loved you."

Was I hoping for a response, for pardon? I don't know. What I got was that same blank stare, that closed door.

I took the high road instead of the coward's way. So much for integrity and authenticity and all those noble concepts my shrink keeps talking about. I told the truth— the whole truth—and she didn't believe me. Not a word of it.

PART THREE

Reconciliation

. . .

I am a woman
whose life is built
on words,
and yet
some truths
resist both voice and pen.
A touch,
a kiss,
a glance,
a hand reached out—
these are the languages
I must learn,
or else
die silent
and alone.

· 22 ·

Somehow Dell Haley found it in her heart to forgive me. I don't know how it happened. We never talked about Chase's infidelity again, but on Christmas Eve Boone called me with bad news and good news. First, he said that because of the robbery, Dell didn't have money for the rent and was going to be evicted. Second, she had decided to go out with a bang, a big Christmas dinner at the Heartbreak Cafe for all her friends. And I was invited.

I was invited.

I am Word Woman, and yet I marvel at how a single word can make such a difference.

Lonely.

Loved.

Rejected.
Invited.

Of course, getting away from Mama on Christmas Day wasn't as easy as I'd hoped. She drank some wine and got all maudlin and weepy on me, a conversation I was sure she'd regret when she was sober. All about how everybody loved Daddy more than they did her, including her own children. How no one wanted to be with her on Christmas (what am I, chopped giblets?). In summary, how disappointed she was in all of us and in life in general.

I'd had about all I could take and was trying to stifle the scream when she said she thought she'd go lie down and rest for a while.

As soon as I heard her bedroom door click shut, I bolted for the car.

I once had a long discussion with a counselor about the subject of forgiveness. Not the white-haired old fool who sent me home to Belladonna, but a red-haired younger fool who probably would have hauled me back to Chulahatchie years earlier, if I'd just stuck around long enough.

Anyway, the therapist du jour (her name was Erin, I think) seemed to have learned her trade at the International College of Counseling and Carnival Acts. I always came out of her sessions feeling like I'd spent fifty minutes with my back up against a bull's-eye, while she threw knives in my direction, trying to see how close she could get without drawing blood.

On one such occasion the subject was forgiveness. Erin urged me toward forgiving my mother. By "forgive," she didn't mean "condone" or "accept," but simply acknowledge my mother's history and limitations, and realize she hadn't intended the hurt she caused me.

"You'll never be free of her control over you until you learn to forgive her," Erin said.

"I'll never be free of her until she's dead," I said.

It was not my most shining moment, but it was honest. Brutally honest.

Erin smiled and held my gaze. "Are you sure you want to wait that long?" she said.

Damn. This is why I hate therapists.

But I digress. I was talking about forgiveness.

I walked into the Heartbreak Cafe on Christmas Day afternoon with my gut trembling and my whole body weak with anxiety. Dell looked up and smiled.

That was all. Just smiled.

I squeezed into a space next to Imani, and the little girl grabbed my hand and pulled me down to whisper a secret in my ear.

"When I grow up," she said, "I want to be a beauty queen, just like you."

I fumbled in my bag and brought up the rhinestone crown from my Miss Ole Miss days. "Then you shall have your wish," I said and settled the glittering tiara on her head. "I crown you Queen of Corn Casserole. Duchess of Dressing. Princess of Pumpkin. Monarch of Muffins."

Imani began to laugh. Everyone cheered and clapped.

I looked around, and the anxiety I'd been feeling since my last conversation with Dell drained away, leaving behind a warmth like the finest cognac going down.

If this is what forgiveness feels like, maybe Erin wasn't so far off the mark, after all.

Boxing Day.

That's what the British call the day after Christmas. It has something to do with opening gifts, I think. At Belladonna, it meant keeping out of Mama's way so as to avoid getting boxed.

She never hit us, of course. Not physically. Mama had much more effective means of bullying us into submission. A word, a look, a gesture of disapproval was enough to send me belly-up, figuratively speaking, like a cowed dog waiting for a reprimand but hoping, always hoping, for a pat of affirmation.

Once Christmas Day was officially "over" and she had nothing else to look forward to, Mama went into a depression that spilled like battery acid onto all of us. We never knew exactly what brought it on—our failure to purchase exactly the right gift, perhaps; a real or imagined slight; a blot on the picture-perfect *Southern Living* Christmas; or a vague and undefined sense of being underappreciated. Whatever the cause, she'd take to her bed with exhaustion and a migraine for a couple of days.

Around the twenty-seventh or twenty-eighth she'd re-appear, muttering (just loud enough for everyone to hear) about how the clutter was getting to her and how much work she had to do to get the decorations put away for an-other year. "This house is driving me crazy," she'd say, so predictably I could set my watch by her. "Doesn't anybody else care?"

And so, of course, we'd all get up and dash around, catering to Mama's need for order, just so we wouldn't have to listen to the litany of complaints any longer than absolutely necessary.

This year, while Mama nursed her Boxing Day head-ache, I decided to cut her off at the pass and go ahead and put away the decorations. There wasn't nearly as much as usual, given our minimalist two-person Christmas. And besides, it gave me something to do with my hands while I let my thoughts swirl around a cloud bank of unformed ideas building on the horizon of my mind.

Once upon a time my shrink, the old white-haired fool—and, come to think of it, the young redheaded fool, too—had suggested, none too gently, that I lived as if I were powerless to control the direction of my own destiny.

My initial reaction to this was, "Duh!"

Nobody controlled their own destiny. You just took what you had coming and lived with the fallout.

Now I wasn't so satisfied with that conviction. By that philosophy, Dell somehow deserved to be evicted and lose everything she'd worked for to build the Heartbreak Cafe. God or fate or the stars had aligned against her, and there was nothing anyone could do.

Maybe Boone was right. Maybe there were simply rhythms of life, and the power of the individual lay not in controlling outcomes but in generating positive responses in the midst of challenge.

I took the ornaments off the tree, wrapped them in tissue, and packed them away in their box. Then I wrestled the naked Christmas tree out the door and down the sidewalk to the street. I was just dragging it off the curb into the gutter for pickup, when I heard a sound.

A faint jingle. Like the sound of the bell over the door of the Heartbreak Cafe.

I turned the tree over and felt in its branches. And there it was—the inevitable "last ornament," the one that hides itself until everything is put away. I extricated it from the tangle of limbs and held it up. It was a small crystal angel holding a tiny brass bell that tinkled when it moved.

I held up the angel and shook it, and I felt an unfamiliar delight flood through me on the pure, clear tone of the little bell. A weak December sun caught the crystal in its light and broke into a prism of colors. And just as suddenly, the clouds broke inside my mind, and a ray of insight came shining through.

Dell Haley was my hero, my inspiration—a strong, capable woman who had made the best out of a difficult situation, who had forged a new life and a new calling out of the ashes. I had hurt her terribly by my selfishness, and even my ignorance was no excuse. I couldn't give her back her husband or her marriage or the life she once had, but I had to do something. And I knew what it was.

Something tangible. Something real.

It might not work. But I had to try. For Dell's sake, and for the sake of my own soul.

Holding the angel aloft like a trophy, I ran back into the house, jerked up the phone, and dialed Boone Atkins's number.

He answered on the second ring. "Peach?" he said. "Do I hear bells ringing?"

I laughed. "Boone, have you ever seen *It's a Wonderful Life*?"

"Of course," he said. "Every Christmas."

"Good. Because a prayer is about to be answered, and an angel is about to get its wings."

In the end, we raised over twenty-eight thousand dollars for Dell to put a down payment on the Heartbreak Cafe. No one ever knew that I spearheaded the whole thing—no one except Boone, and I swore him to secrecy. It all came in bits and pieces, fives and tens and twenties, from truck drivers and the guys at Tenn-Tom Plastics and the little old ladies who came in for pie and coffee in the afternoons.

We all loved Dell. We all believed in her. We just didn't believe in ourselves, in our ability to change the future, until we all joined forces to do it together.

Five or ten or twenty dollars means nothing. One candle in a darkened room doesn't give much light. But you put those dollars together, you bring those candles in and light them off that single flame, and you have enough. Enough resources, enough illumination . . .

Enough of everything that matters.

· 23 ·

I sat in the rocker on the back verandah and looked down the broad sweep of lawn that stretched from the rear of the house to the river. The forsythia were blooming their heads off, draping their tentacles across the grass and the bricks of the walkway. The azaleas had begun to show little closed fists of color, and along the riverbank redbuds popped purple against the yellow-green of dogwoods about to open.

I took a deep breath, drew that fragrance into my lungs, and turned my attention back to my journal.

Southern Spring. They ought to bottle it and sell it for a hundred bucks an ounce. There's not a scent like it anywhere else in the universe.

Is it possible I've actually been here a year? Four seasons, twelve months, almost five hundred pages of journaling—memories and insights and angst and anger?

The white-haired old fool ought to be proud. I don't know how much I've grown and deepened in this year, but at least I've survived without resorting to either murder or suicide.

One sign of progress: I hadn't thought about Robert in weeks, until the final divorce papers arrived three days ago. As I signed them and stuffed them back into the return envelope, a wave of recognition flooded over me, an awareness that had been circling around in my brain, buzzing like a June bug looking for a place to land.

Then it settled down in my consciousness, a full-blown epiphany: Robert's divorcing me was less a rejection than a liberation. I never would have left him—I wouldn't have had the courage—but now that it's done, I've become aware of a great weight lifted.

Maybe I should write him a thank-you note. It's what a proper Southern Lady would do, after all, to acknowledge receipt of a gift.

The gift of being open to love, to creativity, to new beginnings. How strange it is, to realize that I was forty-five years old when I came back to Chula-hatchie, and yet I didn't have a clue what love was.

Like some starry-eyed adolescent, I thought it was all about romance and roses and raging hormones. And then I walked into the Heartbreak Cafe and discovered a whole new definition.

Oh, I thought I loved Robert. And he probably thought he loved me, too. Maybe we did love each other, as much as we were able to love. But my friendships with Dell and Boone, Scratch and Alyssa and Imani, have taught me more about real love than I ever imagined.

Even crusty, crazy old Hoot Everett and Purdy Overstreet have caught the bug. They're getting married in two weeks. At the Heartbreak Cafe (where else?).

Love isn't all about irresistible urges and gushy feelings in the moonlight. It's about finding people who value your soul, who help you stay centered, who call you to account, who affirm your intrinsic worth and value. It's about doing the same for them and finding mutuality in relationship.

Maybe someday I'll fall in love again. Maybe at fifty or sixty I'll find the love of my life—or at least the love of this life, this new life. Maybe God or fate or the universe will throw me into the arms of my last best love, the one who will truly see me—scars and cellulite and wrinkles and fault lines and all—and love me for my real self.

Or maybe not. What I do know is that at forty-six,

I'm not nearly as concerned about being old and alone
as I was at forty-five.

The check finally came through, the cashing out of my relationship with Robert. It may be true that you can't put a
price on love, but houses and cars and furniture can all be
split, fifty-fifty.

In the end, Robert kept everything—the 1922 Arts and
Crafts bungalow we'd bought and renovated together, all
the Mission oak furniture I loved, even the artwork. For a
millisecond I wondered how his new girlfriend would like
living in the house I'd created, but the moment passed, and
I discovered I really didn't care. I didn't want any of it. I
just wanted to be done.

True to form, Robert sent me documentation on
everything—the current appraisal on the house, a detailed
estimate of the value of the contents, all very generous, all
very civilized. More than enough for me to start over, to
buy a place of my own and furnish it, to go back to my life
and pick up where I left off.

It was time to go home.

But first I had some important business to attend to.

In college, at the W, I once took a seminar on Flannery
O'Connor. I remember the professor describing her writing process as "finding interesting characters and following them around to see what they'll do." Flannery would
have loved Hoot Everett and Purdy Overstreet. She would
have been at their wedding come hell or high water.

And I wasn't going to miss it, either.

It was April Fool's Day. I won't even comment on the irony of that choice. The cafe was packed with all the people who loved Hoot and Purdy, and a lot of folks who were just downright curious.

A huge two-tiered wedding cake sat in the center of the marble counter, surrounded by an odd assortment of pot-luck dishes in mismatched serving dishes, disposable tins, and Tupperware. I don't know how the nose can discern among such mingled odors, but I caught a whiff of fried chicken, pork barbecue, corn bread, and chocolate.

The minister for the occasion was the Reverend Lily Frasier, the new chaplain at St. Agnes Nursing Home. She was trying her best to maintain order and decorum, but with Hoot and Purdy this was easier said than done.

She barely got out their full names—Herman Melville Everett and Priscilla Mayben Overstreet—before all hell broke loose. I never knew Purdy and I shared the same first name, but I had little time to think about the coincidence. The vows themselves were lost in the chaos. Hoot interrupted Reverend Lily, yelling, "I do!" before she even got the question out. Purdy demanded that she "skip the formalities and get on with it."

In the end it didn't matter one bit. Everybody cheered when Hoot kissed Purdy—he took this as a sign that he ought to keep on going, which he did until she pushed him away and danced him across the room, crooning "I'll Be Seeing You" at the top of her lungs.

I watched it all from my accustomed booth in the back, but on this day I wasn't writing in my journal. There's a time for observing and a time for participating.

Boone and Toni joined me in the booth, and Imani came to sit in my lap. I hadn't told any of them I was leaving Chulahatchie; the timing hadn't seemed quite right, especially today of all days. But I had brought a gift for Imani—the tiara from my reign as Soybean Queen. I put it on her head and kissed her on the cheek.

"You mean I can keep it?" she said. "For all and forever?"

I nodded. "For all and forever."

She hugged me around the middle until I thought I'd never breathe properly again. "I love you, Aunt Peach," she said.

"I love you, too."

It was a good thing the music was so loud. When the tears came, nobody caught me dabbing my eyes on a cocktail napkin. I recovered my composure, read the gold embossing on the napkin, and laughed out loud:

Hoot and Purdy, Old but Not Yet Dead

Five people at Hoot and Purdy's wedding told me I looked beautiful. And I believed them. I *felt* beautiful, in this flowing eggplant-colored dress I'd found at the consignment shop. It concealed most of my figure flaws, but I couldn't have cared less, one way or another.

Hearing it from Boone and Dell and Fart Unger was a sight different from hearing it from Charles Chase—or, rather, Chase Haley. When he said I looked beautiful, I never really believed him. But I was desperate to think myself beautiful again, and he knew it, and he used it.

One of these days the episode with Chase would seem like ancient history, a dim image from a half-forgotten nightmare. I was grateful beyond belief for Dell's forgiveness, but while I waited for the memory to fade, I had to live with the awareness that I was not nearly as good a person as I'd thought myself to be.

I was still musing about it when I turned the corner toward Belladonna and saw the flashing lights.

· 24 ·

There's something strangely anachronistic about police cars and ambulances and fire trucks and bars of red and blue lights clustered around a place like Belladonna. The house was born in a slower time, an era of lamplight and carriages and the clip-clop of horses' hooves. A gentler time—at least for the privileged few who dwelt in these opulent homes. Perhaps not so gentle for the slaves who chopped cotton, or the sharecroppers who took to the land after emancipation. Perhaps not so gentle for the teenage boys on both sides of the line who drained out their blood on the fields at Vicksburg and Sharpsburg and Shiloh.

With images of bullets and bayonets and blood flashing across the back of my brain, I left my Honda at the curb and dashed up the brick sidewalk. Standing on the front verandah with his arms folded across his chest was the last person I wanted to see at the moment: the idiot sheriff who had arrested Scratch last December.

"What happened?" I said. I tried to push by him into the house, but he blocked my way.

"They're bringing her out now." He motioned with his head, and I peered past him to see the EMTs coming out of the parlor with Mama strapped to a rolling gurney. Her eyes were closed and her skin looked pale and clammy. The ludicrous thought flitted through my mind that she couldn't be dead since her face wasn't covered and they had an oxygen mask strapped to her mouth.

This time the sheriff didn't resist as I shoved past him and grabbed hold of the gurney's side rail. "What happened?" I repeated.

The paramedic looked across my mother's body and into my eyes. She was about my age, but she was tan and fit and had the look of a woman who lived with a purpose. I wondered for a millisecond whether she was sizing me up and finding me wanting.

"We think your mother's had a stroke," she said. Her voice was measured and calm, infused with a quiet confidence that caused some of my own anxiety to dissipate. "We're taking her to the hospital now. Perhaps you and her friend could come together."

Her friend?

I looked around. Standing in the big double doorway that led to the parlor was Gladys Dalrymple, whom everyone in the country club set called Gladdie. The woman was further from glad than anyone I had ever known or imagined. Her daughter—named, with equal irony, Dymple—was just like her, a sour-faced girl without a dimple in her whole doughy face, unless you counted that green-persimmon pucker.

Gladdie frowned at me. "This," she hissed, "is all your fault. And after everything that woman's done for you!"

I opened my mouth to respond and shut it again. And then, without giving Gladdie the satisfaction of seeing my confusion and outrage, I spun on my heel and followed the EMTs out the door.

"It wasn't as bad as it might have been," the doctor said. "She's got some paralysis on the left side, and her speech will be difficult for a time, but she's made good progress in the past week. In a couple more days I'll release her to go home. She won't get back everything she's lost, but with therapy and some hard work, she ought to do fine."

He looked down at the chart and then back up at me. "You live with her, is that correct?"

"Yes, but—" I paused. "Only temporarily. I was fixing to move back home as soon as I could find a place."

"And home is—" He consulted the chart again.

"Asheville," I supplied. "North Carolina."

"How far away is that?"

"About ten hours." I felt myself sinking in a quicksand

so profound I might never again feel solid ground beneath my feet.

The doctor shook his head. "She can't be in that big old house alone," he said. "Unless you want to consider assisted living or St. Agnes Nursing Home, she has to have someone with her."

I already knew, of course, who that someone would be. In the week since Mama's stroke, I had talked to Melanie every night and to Harry only once. He was on the beach at Belize or scuba diving the Great Barrier Reef or something. All I got from him was, "You're breaking up; I can't hear you," and "I know you'll do what's best for Mom. I'll call you when I get back to the States."

Melanie, on the other hand, had plenty to say. Since Mama was in no immediate danger, she wasn't going to fly to Mississippi all the way from California, but she sympathized with my plight. "I know it's not your responsibility," she said for the hundredth time, "but you're the one who's there. Mama's got plenty of money. We can hire someone to take care of her. We can set her up in a really nice place where she'll be looked after."

"She doesn't want to leave Belladonna," I said, also for the hundredth time. "You know how much she loves that old house."

"Yeah, I know," Melanie said. She left the other half of the sentence unspoken: *More than she loves you or me.* "But Peach, she's not in a position to make all the decisions anymore. For once in her life she can't get everything she wants."

But she did.

As usual.

Before I brought Mama home, I had a long talk with the banker and then an even longer one with Tildy. Melanie was right about one thing: Mama could afford just about anything she needed or wanted. My daddy had done his job, at least according to the prevailing wisdom of his generation. Money was not going to be an issue. His family would be taken care of.

With that worry relieved, I set about taking charge of Mama's affairs—the power of attorney, financial control of the estate, all the legalities I'd need to run the house, write checks, pay bills, and see that Mama was cared for.

As soon as I had power of the checkbook, I sat Tildy down and laid out my plan. "I need you, Tildy," I said. "And Mama needs you, too. It's going to be hard for her not to be in control—"

Tildy gave a wicked grin. "You reckon?"

"Yeah, I reckon." It was the first time I'd laughed since the night I'd come home to those flashing lights, and it felt like a deep breath after being underwater. Oxygen flooded my brain cells, and everything seemed to come a little clearer.

And so it was decided. Tildy would come every day in time to get Mama up and bathed and dressed and to get breakfast for us. She'd stay until three thirty or four, which would give me a chance to run errands and go to the Piggly Wiggly and maybe get a little time to myself. She'd leave supper on the stove. On weekends I was on my own.

"The doctor warned me that Mama isn't going to be her old self," I told Tildy. "So we have to be prepared. The stroke may have affected the portions of her brain that deal with social filters—you know, impulse control and tact, that kind of thing. We may find that she blurts out whatever comes into her mind without considering how it makes other people feel."

"In other words, Miss Donna's gonna be *exactly* her old self, only more so," Tildy said.

I couldn't argue with that, even if I had been so inclined.

On the afternoon I brought Mama home from the hospital, every chair on the front verandah was filled with folks waiting for us to show up. From my vantage point as I pulled in the driveway, it looked a little bit like the Hatfields and McCoys, or maybe the Union vs. the Confederacy.

I got out, helped Mama into the collapsible wheelchair, and rolled her up onto the porch.

On the left sat Boone, Scratch, and Dell's friend Fart Unger, along with Dell, Alyssa, and Imani. Fart was holding his toolbox, so I was pretty sure he was responsible for the ramp that took up half of the broad steps up to the verandah. It was easily wide enough for a wheelchair and had a sturdy handrail.

Dell Haley perched on a rocker with an enormous cardboard box propped across the wide wooden arms of the chair. Even with the tinfoil still on, I was pretty sure I could smell chicken and ham pie, applesauce cake, and fresh corn bread and collard greens.

Alyssa sat with Imani in her lap. The child held a huge bouquet of spring flowers. At a nudge from her mother, she came forward and laid the bouquet in Mama's lap. "These are for you, Miz Rondell," she said then ducked her head and sidled over to me for a hug.

"She can't talk very well right now," I explained to Imani. "But thank you so much; the flowers are lovely."

No one on the right side of the porch had moved. Gladys Dalrymple and her daughter, Dymple, looked like they'd been frozen into statues by the White Witch of Narnia. Two more of Mama's country club cronies were there as well—razor-thin look-alikes, with platinum teased hair and bony knuckles knobbled with diamonds and rubies. I had met them, I knew, but even if I had been able to call up their names at the moment, I wouldn't have been able to tell you which was which.

What I did remember was what Gladys had said to me the night Mama went to the hospital: *This is all your fault.* In the trauma and anxiety of Mama's stroke and the stress of being thrust into the role of caregiver, I had completely forgotten about it until now.

Gladys, obviously, had not forgotten. She glared at me across the empty space between us, looking from me to Mama and then to Scratch, Dell, and the others.

My training as a Southern Lady kicked into overdrive. "Please come in," I said to them all. "Y'all are so gracious to support Mama this way. She's very tired, as you might imagine, but I'll get her settled and then we can all have coffee."

Alyssa cut a glance across to Gladys and, almost protectively, put an arm around Imani and drew her close. "Perhaps we should come back another day," she said in a quiet voice. "Peach, you call us if you need anything. We'll see you soon."

There was a flurry of hugs and kisses, and some hasty good-byes, and all the Heartbreak Cafe folks were gone. I was left facing the Dalrymples and the bleached blonde twins.

"*That*," Gladys Dalrymple said with a huff of outrage, "is why your mama is in this wheelchair." She pointed in the direction of town, where Dell's car and Fart's truck were just disappearing around the bend. "Surely you know better, Priscilla, than to consort with such people! Surely your mama raised you better than this!"

I didn't invite them in a second time. Instead, I pushed Mama's wheelchair across the threshold and turned at the doorway.

"Cows are raised," I said. "Cabbages are raised. Southern Ladies are *brought up*."

While she was still gaping at me, I shut the door to Belladonna in her face.

"And the name," I muttered to the closed front door, "is not Priscilla. It's Peach. *Peach*."

Mama reached up with her good right hand and squeezed my fingers.

"Pee," she said. "Na piss. Pee."

· 25 ·

Over the years I've seen a lot of different looks from my mother. I've seen her angry plenty of times, and petulant, and demanding. I've seen her sneaky and manipulative and self-absorbed and whiny. I've seen her as an exultant winner and an ungracious, bad-tempered loser. I've watched her, in T. S. Eliot's words, "put on a face to meet the faces that you meet," and recognized all too often the polite and icy smile that masks a seething disapproval.

But never this emptiness, like a deflated balloon. Never this vacancy, this void, this eerie stillness.

Wherever Tildy and I position her, she stays—in

the bed, on the sofa, at the dining room table, in the wheelchair. She's like a mannequin in a display window advertising strokes for sale.

The doctor says it will take some time for her to begin to come back to us, that depression is a normal response to this kind of loss, and that we just have to be patient. All those years I wished she would just shut up and go away . . . now she has, and how do I learn to cope with it?

"Peach?"

I looked up to see Dell and Scratch standing over me.

"Are we interrupting?"

I closed the journal with the pen still inside to hold my place and noticed how few blank pages were left. I supposed I'd have to drive up to Tupelo in a week or two and scout out the office supply stores for a refill.

I shrugged and motioned for them to sit. "Just trying to sort out things with Mama," I said. "I've got a telephone session with my counselor tomorrow afternoon."

They were well aware of my ongoing relationship with the old white-haired fool, of course. I had long since given up any pretense with these friends. I simply didn't have the energy for it.

A fragment of memory flashed across my mind—an old episode of *Star Trek*, in which a Romulan vessel is attacking the *Enterprise*. "They can't stay invisible forever, Captain," Spock says. "The cloaking device is draining their energy banks."

Indeed. Staying hidden was immensely draining, and what would it accomplish, anyway? They were smart enough to know when I was faking. And for the first time in my life I had friends who'd prefer to see me real and ragged rather than falsely cheerful.

Dell sat down on the opposite side of the booth, and Scratch pulled a chair up from another table. "You okay?" Dell said.

"Yeah. Just tired. Exhausted, really. And worried."

"How's your mama?" Scratch said. "Any change?"

"Not much. She'll eat when we feed her and doesn't protest when we move her, but that's about it. She doesn't even try to talk. I don't know what to do. Last night I thought I heard a noise, and when I went in to check on her, she was just lying there in the dark staring up at the ceiling."

Dell looked at me, the kind of look that seemed to pierce right through to the other side. "Even when you're doing the right thing, it's hard when you feel trapped."

My gut twisted. "What do you mean?"

She propped her chin on one hand and gazed at me. "You were all ready to go home, to pick up your life where you left it, and then this happened."

I stared at her. "How did you know? I didn't tell anyone. I'd only just made the decision when Mama . . ."

Dell shrugged. "It made sense. The divorce was final, and the division of property had been taken care of. You didn't need to be here any longer. In Chulahatchie, I mean. Living with your mama."

She didn't have to say the rest: *You didn't need us anymore.*

I felt reproach where she had intended none; it came not from her, but from deep inside of me.

The truth was, I had intended to do just that—go back to Asheville, pick up my life, and get on with whatever the future held, until my year of exile in Chulahatchie faded to a dim memory, the shadow of a dream.

I remember once telling my therapist that mental health was vastly overrated. Why do all that work to become self-aware when living in denial is infinitely easier and more comfortable?

Now, when I stepped outside myself, I saw something that shocked me, something that rattled the bars of my cage and made me shudder with revulsion and disbelief. Could I possibly be that self-centered—perfectly content to accept the love and support these friends had offered, and then when I didn't need them any longer, walk away without a backward glance? Could I possibly care only about what I needed, about what I wanted?

Could I possibly be that much like . . .

My mother?

And what if—

The idea sneaked up behind me and swatted me upside

the head so hard it left me weak in the knees with my ears ringing.

What if *they* needed *me*?

I was probably going to regret this for the rest of my life, but the idea sprang from my head fully formed like Athena, the goddess of wisdom; like a vision or a calling. I couldn't have denied it to save my sorry soul.

I paused at the front porch and knelt down, taking both of Imani's hands in my own. "Honey," I said, "you need to understand that my mama is very sick. She's been in the hospital and she's weak, and she might not respond to you—or she might act as if she's angry. Do you understand?"

Imani gazed at me and nodded solemnly. "Daddy explained it to me. Your mama's had a stroke and you've been taking care of her, and that's why I haven't seen you very much."

"That's right." I pulled her close and felt the warmth of her little body against mine, the softness of her brown cheek under my fingers. "I've missed you."

"I missed you, too." She looked up at me. "I know you're sad about your mama," she said. "But you don't have to do it all by yourself. You've got friends who love you, Aunt Peach. We'll all help."

She reached into her pink backpack and brought out a battered copy of *The Secret Garden*, the one I had given her, the one with full-page color illustrations. "It's my favorite book," she said. "I thought maybe I could read it to your mama."

Tears welled up in my throat. "That's real sweet, honey." I forced a smile, but inside I was cringing. Even half paralyzed with a stroke, my mother was fully capable of eating this precious child for breakfast.

"Okeydokey," I said at last. "Let's go on in."

I opened the front door and we went inside. Imani paused in the foyer, looking up at the massive stairway that curved up to the second floor. "This reminds me of Granddaddy's house," she whispered.

"Did you like living with your granddaddy?" I asked.

"It was all right. He bought me lots of things, but he almost never played with me because he was working all the time." She grinned. "I like living at Aunt Dell's river camp a whole lot better. Daddy takes me fishing, and we dig for crawdads."

I understood perfectly. "I grew up here," I told her. "Later I'll take you up to my room and let you play with my big dollhouse. But right now there's someone you need to meet."

I pushed through the swinging door into the kitchen, where Tildy was drizzling white icing onto a coffee cake that smelled deliciously of butter and cinnamon.

"Don't even ask," she said with her back still turned toward the door. "It's your mama's favorite, and nobody gets so much as a crumb until she says so. I thought I might be able to tempt her to eat something."

She turned around, grinning, and her eyes widened at the sight of Imani. "Well, who do we have here?"

Imani went suddenly shy at the sight of this six-foot black woman towering over her. I nudged her forward. "This is Imani Greer," I said. "Imani, say hello to Mrs. Matilda Brown. We call her Tildy."

Imani mustered up her courage and held out a hand. "How are you, Miz Tildy? I'm very pleased to meet you."

Tildy shook her hand. "Likewise. And to what do we owe the honor of this visit?"

"I'm here to see Miz Rondell," Imani said. "I've come to help her feel better."

Tildy threw back her head and laughed. "A miracle worker in our midst! How old are you, child?"

"I just turned nine years old." Imani gave her a curious look. "Don't you believe in miracles, Miss Tildy?"

"I wouldn't know. I reckon I've never seen one."

"Maybe you *have* seen one," the child said, "and just didn't know it. Daddy says sometimes coincidences are just miracles in disguise."

"Mercy, mercy," Tildy said to me. "A miracle worker *and* a philosopher." She leaned down to Imani's level. "Have *you* ever seen a miracle?"

"Yes."

"And just exactly what kind? Water turned to wine?

Somebody walking on water? Lazarus being raised from the dead?"

Imani giggled. "No."

"Then what, pray tell?"

"Mama and Daddy being together again," Imani said.

Tildy straightened up and put her hands on her hips. "Cain't argue with that kind of logic."

"Where's Mama?" I asked.

"On the back verandah. I brought her out; thought maybe the fresh air would do her good. It's such a shame. Your mama always loved the spring, and this is one of the prettiest ones I can remember in a long, long time. Too bad she can't appreciate it."

I left Tildy to finish the coffee cake and took Imani out back. Mama was sitting in one of the rocking chairs, staring out into the yard toward the river. Her good right foot pushed against the bricks of the porch to keep the chair moving; her paralyzed left leg simply flopped with the motion, and her left hand, drawn up in a claw, lay motionless in her lap.

"Mama?" I said.

She turned her head in my direction. Her face looked normal on the right, but on the left her eye sagged and her jaw drooped. A thin string of saliva dripped onto her chest from the left side of her mouth; she couldn't feel it.

The rocking stopped. I saw her good eye rake me up and down as I stood there holding the hand of a little black girl. I felt disapproval roll off of her like waves headed for shore. I was just about to take Imani and go, when the child broke away from me and ran toward Mama.

Without waiting to be invited, she climbed up into Mama's lap, pulled a tissue out of the box on the table, and wiped away the spittle. Then she took her hand and stroked the left side of Mama's face—gently, tenderly.

"Miz Rondell," she whispered, "my name's Imani, and if you'll let me, I'd like to be your friend." She smiled into Mama's ruined face. "I brought a book for us to read." She pulled it out of her backpack and showed it to Mama. "*The Secret Garden*. It's all about a girl who needs a family, and a sick boy who gets healed because his friends love him."

Imani wriggled her little body into a comfortable position and laid her head on my mother's chest with the top of her head fitted under Mama's chin. I held my breath. Mama hesitated for a fraction of a second, then her right arm came around the child and held her close, and the right side of her face twitched into a half smile.

Her right foot jerked, tapped on the bricks of the verandah, and then pushed. The chair began to rock once more. And then I heard it—a low humming. It took a moment for me to recognize the tune, to dredge it up from the depths of my memory.

It was a lullaby. The one my mama used to sing to me.

· 26 ·

Imani came every day after that. Tildy's prophecy proved true—the child was both a philosopher and a miracle worker.

Mama spent most of her time now on the back verandah, watching as April shook out her multihued skirts around grass-green crinolines. The whole universe seemed to dip and sway in the ancient dance of veneration, celebrating the return of spring.

When she wasn't sitting, rocking, smiling, humming to herself, Mama was working. Physical therapy, speech therapy, occupational therapy—she did it all, without a word of complaint. Her brain retrained itself to wrap around the language lost to the stroke. By inches her strength returned, until she could get around by herself with the aid of a walker.

Every afternoon at two thirty, she'd haul herself out to the porch and settle herself in the rocking chair, waiting for school to let out, gripping Imani's copy of *The Secret Garden*. What the two of them talked about was beyond my understanding. It remained their secret, and though the temptation was almost unbearable, I never interfered, never eavesdropped, never asked. I did hear Imani call my mother GranDonna once, and I saw the tender embrace as they said good-bye.

I should have wept for joy. But instead something inside roared and flamed, a fury I never knew was in me. I hadn't expected to glimpse such intimacy, hadn't known my mother had it in her. And my reaction stunned and shamed me.

Why?

I can't get past the question. It haunts me, rubs me raw, like a rash I can't rid myself of. How can my mother, who has spent her life criticizing me and making me feel as if there is something fundamentally wrong about me, now give herself so freely and lovingly to a child not her own? A black child. A child who, before the stroke, she would have crossed the street to avoid. Now she rocks Imani on her lap and braids her hair, sings to her, holds her as if that warm little body were a life preserver that could keep her from drowning.

I ought to be glad—glad that Mama is alive, glad that this dear child, whom I love as if she were my own, could be the catalyst to bring my mother back to herself.

Isn't that what I wanted? Isn't it what I hoped for, when I brought Imani to Belladonna that first day?

True, I was multitasking, finding a way to spend time with Imani without neglecting Mama. But didn't I hope that somehow Mama would respond to her, the way Alzheimer's patients respond to little children or therapy dogs? Didn't I pray that this would be the outcome—if not a miracle, then at least a glimmer of light in the darkness, a sliver of moon, the wink of a star?

I'm ashamed of my reaction, but I simply can't help it. It makes me furious to think that my own mother couldn't find it in her heart to love and cherish me, and yet she can do it for Imani. What gives her the right to withhold love from her own daughter and offer it to a stranger? How is it that I am so unlovable?

The white-haired old fool would probably say that we've finally dug down to the core issue, the essential fault line in the foundation of my being. He'd consider it a great victory. But he's not hanging on to the mountain by his fingernails, grappling for dear life (or not so dear). I'm the one who has to sit by and see my own mother betraying me with every lopsided smile and one-armed hug she gives to another little girl.

As a child I resented my mother's critical spirit and wished she could be loving and accepting and encouraging and approachable, the way some of my friends' mothers were. As an adult, I backed away from her, trying to shield myself, to protect my heart from being hurt any more. I thought I had dealt with the pain and that the only thing left was the anger.

Now I realize: The anger is the pain. Anger is nothing more than a smoke screen for hurt and fear. It keeps the pain at bay, keeps the fear pushed down. But at the end of the tunnel, there it is again. If I stay good and mad, I don't have to admit my vulnerabilities, don't have to face the truth that I'm afraid and wounded and that those wounds have never really healed.

And how could they heal? They've never been exposed to light and air. They've been bandaged up, scabbed, grafted over. But the poison remains, festering below the surface, oozing, spreading its tentacles into other relationships.

How might my marriage to Robert have been different, better, if I had been healthier, more honest, more self-aware? How much of my anger with Mama seeped into that underground stream and tainted the waters? How much of my childhood angst kept me from finding joy and contentment as an adult?

Always, always, I wanted to belong. I wanted to

be loved and cared for; I wanted to relax. But it never happened. Even when I was loved, I couldn't believe it, couldn't rest in it. I was always afraid, always picking at the old scars. Always looking for proof—some proof my mother never managed to give.

Now a switch has flipped inside her, and she has suddenly turned into GranDonna. Tender. Loving. Affectionate. And I find myself wondering: Where's the pod, and what have the aliens done with my real mother?

And then I ask myself: If I found the real Mama, would I want her back?

"I told you," the doctor said. "You have to expect changes. The part of her brain that filters her thoughts and emotions has been affected. She'll likely just say and do whatever she wants without any regard to how it will affect other people. She'll have no tact, no social grace."

I stared at him. "But she's . . . well, not herself."

"She *is* herself," he said. "She's probably more herself than she's ever been."

"But that makes no sense. I expected her to be—" I paused. "Well, to tell the truth I expected her to be mean and crabby and hypercritical. Like she's always been."

He shrugged. "Your mother's doing well, Peach. Her speech is less slurred, and although she'll probably always have some paralysis in the left side, she's making a remarkable comeback. All I can tell you is what we've discov-

ered in cases like hers: The stroke strips away the facade.
It changes people."

No shit, I thought.

The question was, could I deal with the changes?

As I expected, my therapist was ecstatic over my break-
through. To me it felt more like a break*down*, but I didn't
bother to correct him. I just let him rave on about how
much I was learning and how far I'd come. He'd learn the
real truth sooner or later. Maybe a lot later. Maybe never.

If I thought it was difficult living with the old critical
Mama when I first came back to Chulahatchie after the
divorce, it was nothing to living with this new improved
Mama. All the hard edges were gone, and nothing was left
but the soft inner core. I saw the light click on in Mama's
eyes every time Imani showed up, a light mirrored in the
little girl's face.

The mother I never had and the child I always wanted.
They had found each other, and I had lost both of them.

"Aunt Peach," Imani said one afternoon as she was
leaving, "are you all right?"

I didn't look her in the eye. I couldn't. "What do you
mean?"

She took my hand and pulled me down beside her on
the front steps of Belladonna, next to Fart's masterpiece of
a ramp. It was late afternoon; the sun was setting behind
the house, and the front verandah had been shaded for

several hours. I felt the chill of the bricks seeping through the fabric of my jeans, and I shivered.

"Isn't your daddy expecting you at the Heartbreak Cafe?" I asked.

"He knows I'm here," Imani said. "If I'm not at the cafe when he's ready to go home, he'll come and find me." She spoke these words with absolute certainty, secure in the knowledge of her father's love and his ability to protect her. I envied her the fearlessness that came with such a sense of safety. If truth be told, I envied a lot of things about Imani.

"Are you all right?" she repeated.

"I'm fine," I lied. "Why do you ask?"

"I don't know. You seem . . . well, different, somehow. You're here, but it feels like you've gone away."

I bit my lip and looked away. This bright, perceptive child did not have the language of a therapist and couldn't talk about me being emotionally absent, but she hammered the nail home anyway.

"I've just been . . ." I groped for a word. "Busy," I said.

"I know. GranDonna told me. She says you've got a lot on your mind."

"My mother said that? To you?"

Imani nodded. "We talk about lots of things. She misses you." The child paused. "I do, too."

It was such a simple, honest statement—Imani's truth, uncolored by pretense or guile.

I couldn't speak my own truth to this innocent child, couldn't say, *Mama can't miss what she's never really known.* Instead I said, "I miss you, too."

She caught the difference and cocked her head the way an intelligent and curious puppy will do. "Remember when we first came to Chulahatchie?" she said. "When Daddy and Mama first found each other again?"

"Of course I remember." I took her hand. "That was when I met you."

"I was afraid—of Daddy, because he was so big and strange, and of all the newness, and of not knowing what was going to happen. And you told me I didn't have to like him, but I should at least give him a chance."

I looked down at her. "I'd forgotten I said that."

She nodded. "Well, maybe that's what you should do."

Scratch pulled up to the curb in his pickup truck and tapped the horn. Imani waved to him, got to her feet, then turned and flung herself into my arms.

"I love you, Aunt Peach," she whispered in my ear. "And so does GranDonna."

She pulled away, slung her pink Power Rangers back-pack over her shoulder, and went skipping down the walk to where her Daddy stood waiting.

· 27 ·

"Pee," Mama said.

I looked up from my journal. After Imani left, I had joined my mother on the back verandah, where we sat encapsulated in our individual bubbles, with nothing to say to one another. It wasn't the companionable quiet of two people who loved and understood each other, but the rigid silence of statues carved in stone, of enemies taking each other's measure out of the corner of their eyes.

The setting sun slanted over the Tombigbee, its lengthening rays laying down a path of gold and green from the high riverbank all the way up the lawn to my feet. It felt like an invitation to play, to shuck off my shoes and run barefoot through the grass and over the embankment into the slow-moving water.

But I didn't. Grown-ups didn't go throwing themselves, fully clothed, into the river on a whim.

"Pee," Mama said again.

I was just about to call for Tildy when I realized it was nearly five thirty. Tildy was long gone and wouldn't be back until Monday morning. The weekend was mine to deal with. Mine alone.

I sighed and heaved myself to my feet. "All right, Mama, come on; I'll help you."

I brought the walker around to the front of her rocking chair and hoisted her up to lean on the bars. She narrowed her good eye and gave me an appraising look.

"Na piss. Pee," she said.

The words jogged a memory somewhere inside my head—it was the same thing she said to me the day she came home, after I sent Gladys and Dymple Dalrymple packing. She had patted my hand and said, "Pee. Na piss. Pee."

"Yeah, yeah, Mama," I said. "We're going. Come on."

I guided her to the downstairs bathroom, settled her on the toilet, and stepped outside to give her a bit of privacy. As I stood listening at the partially open door, it struck me as ludicrous that I had to help her go to the bathroom but would still turn my back so as not to embarrass her.

I waited. No tinkle of peeing. I leaned closer. "Mama? You all right?"

A sound reached my ears, a strangled sob, like the cry of a wounded animal. I pushed the door open. There Mama stood, leaning on the walker with her panties bunched down around her knees, struggling with her good right hand to pull them up one side at a time.

Time seemed to stop. I took in the scene like a living tableau: Mama, always dressed to the nines with perfect hairdo and makeup, now reduced to wearing a snap-front cotton housedress and tennis shoes, her face bare and wrinkled and soft as old flannel, her perm grown out and her roots undyed.

The tears she couldn't shed lodged in my own throat, and I tried in vain to swallow them down. "It's okay, Mama. I'll help," I said in a whisper.

"*No!*" she yelled. She shook her head from side to side, and the movement reminded me of a caged tiger I saw once at the zoo.

I held up both hands. "All right, all right. You just take your time."

She slammed the bathroom door in my face and finally, after what seemed an interminable time, opened it again and shuffled out. I followed her back to the verandah. The sun was setting in earnest now, a blaze of orange and pink and purple clouds that arched above us through the branches of the trees.

The evening had grown chilly. I ducked back into the house, retrieved an afghan from the den, and pulled it around Mama's shoulders. She paid no attention, but rather glared at me out of her one good eye.

"Liffen," she said. "Wee hadda tall."

I gave her a stare that must have been as blank as my brain. I had no idea what she wanted.

She rolled her eye and pointed with her right hand to her ear. *"Liffen!"* she repeated, louder this time, the way you yell at a person who speaks a different language, as if volume alone might bridge the communication gap.

It seemed the ultimate irony. Mama and I hadn't spoken the same language in years. Why start now?

She leaned forward and grabbed my left hand with her right. "Pee," she said.

I exhaled heavily. "You just went to pee."

With a resounding smack, she slapped my hand. "Fay ashension," she commanded, and although the words didn't entirely register, I knew that tone of voice. I'd heard it all my life.

"Pay attention?" I repeated. "All right, Mama, I'm listening."

Listen. *Liffen.* We have to talk.

I hadn't been *liffening.* I hadn't been *faying ashension.* But apparently nine-year-old Imani Greer had, because she and Mama managed to communicate just fine.

Mama looked intently into my eyes. "Pee," she said. "Not Piss."

I shrugged and shook my head.

"Peeee—ch. Not Piss—illa," she repeated, trying harder. "Gaddie caw Pee Piss," she went on. "But Pee na Piss. Gaddie'sh fool."

When I was a child, I'd sit in front of the Christmas tree

and let my eyes slide out of focus so that my whole vision was filled with multicolored sparkling light. Now I listened that way, watching my mother's lopsided face, letting my mind unfocus so that I could hear what she meant rather than what she said.

Gladys Dalrymple. She was talking about Gladdie being a fool, calling me Priscilla when the name that fit me was Peach.

Mama had never called me Peach before in her life, and now she squeezed my hand and said, "I sorry, Pee."

"You don't have anything to be sorry for," I said. We both knew it was a lie, but it slid past the truth meter on a slippery wave of emotion.

"You know why I name you Pissilla?" Mama asked.

I shook my head.

"Pissilla Owerstreet," she said. "Sheesh a good friend. Like a big sister. A minnow."

"A minnow?" I repeated. "You mean a mentor?"

Mama nodded.

"You're talking about Purdy Overstreet? That old showgirl who just married Hoot Everett?"

Mama grinned, and even the left side of her face turned up just a little bit. "She unnerstood me, in a way your granmamma GiGi never did."

I was beginning to comprehend her words more clearly, but I couldn't believe what I was hearing.

"Wait a minute. You and GiGi were inseparable. The two of you were just alike."

"Not alike," Mama said. "Jus' want to please her. Try hard, but—" She shrugged, as if to say my grandmother was impossible to please. "Pissilla unnerstood me, an' I letter down."

My mother lowered her head and stared at the bricks of the verandah floor. "Sush a waste," she murmured, so low that I could barely hear her. "All those years tryin' to do what she wanted—the pageants, the country club, ever'thing."

I waited, hoping for the full apology I had longed for all my life. The admission that she'd been a bad mother, that she'd been self-absorbed and emotionally absent, that she hadn't been there when I needed her, hadn't accepted me for who I was.

But it didn't come.

She turned her face back toward the river and stared out into the waning light of sunset. And in that moment I saw what she saw. Not the closing of a day, but the ending of a life. A life crowded with other people's expectations, guided by principles and priorities not her own.

I saw Melanie turning her back and crossing her arms in adolescent defiance; Harry standing motionless as a boulder in the river, letting the flow of family wash around him and never being moved; myself pulling on Mama's skirts, demanding attention. I saw Daddy going about his business with important clients; saw GiGi shaking a warning finger in Mama's face; saw Grandpa Chick sneaking a slug from a hip flask when nobody was looking.

Where were Mama's dreams, in this life now gone? Where were her ambitions, her hopes and joys and connections? Where were her regrets, her unfulfilled longings, her visions of a future?

Where, in this claustrophobic crush of otherness, did she even have a chance to breathe? I had only a brief glimpse of her reality, and it was enough to send me bolting for the nearest exit.

And then another truth rose briefly to the surface and sank again, the final wave of a soul going down for the last time:

She did the best she could.

Maybe not what I would have wished for myself, or for Melanie, or for Harry. Maybe not what would please my grandmother GiGi, or impress Daddy, or pacify Chick, or earn her a trophy as Mother of the Year. Certainly not what she'd want engraved on her tombstone, but reality nevertheless.

She did the best she could.

A sound pulled me out of my reverie. A quiet whimper. I looked over at my mother, now a silhouette in the fading light. She was crying. Rocking, shivering, clutching the afghan around her with her good right hand, leaning forward as if to follow the last rays of sunset into darkness.

Raging against the dying of the light.

· 28 ·

I'd like to say that from that day forward, I thought more about Mama than I did about myself—that I considered her feelings, understood her better, made a concerted effort to slog through the tangled swamp of past hurt and relate to her as one adult to another.

I'd like to say that.

But inner transformation is about honesty, about getting to the core of my real feelings, and if I'm going to do that, I have to admit that I didn't turn into Mother Teresa after one blazing vision on the Damascus Road. And yes, I know I'm mixing my metaphors, but I absolutely cannot relate to Paul, that great Apostle of Chauvinism, and I'm sure as hell not going to use him as my image of epiphany.

I will say this: Once I started listening, I heard more than I'd bargained for.

Somebody (I forget who; probably one of the myriad therapists that came and went over the years) told me that when you squeeze a lemon, you don't get grape jelly. I take this to mean that when life brings on the pressure, what you really are on the inside comes out.

The doctor warned me. He said that because of the stroke, Mama would have no social filters. She might respond like a person who's had a bit too much to drink, when the walls come down and the inhibitions get stripped away.

I interpreted this in the same way Tildy did, that Mama would become more critical, more demanding, more self-centered and narcissistic.

Instead, the stroke opened up a place in her I never expected to see. And what came out of Mama shocked the living daylights out of me.

"Pee," Mama called.

I came out onto the back verandah wiping my hands on a dish towel. "Dinner's almost ready," I said. "They'll be here any minute. We're having ham and black-eyed peas and collard greens and corn bread. Just like you wanted."

"Peas make me fart," she said.

"I thought you liked black-eyed peas."

"Dinn't say I dinn't like 'em," she said. "Said they make me fart."

"All right. Well, Mama, if we could just not talk about farting at the dinner table, that would be great. We're having company, you know."

Another of my brilliant notions, suggesting that Mama might want to have a few friends over. I figured we'd have a little midafternoon tea with the country club girls, an hour at most, with cucumber sandwiches and lemon squares. Nothing elaborate, nothing labor-intensive.

Instead, we ended up doing dinner for eight on a Saturday night when Tildy wasn't there to help out. It was all Mama's idea, or an idea she and Imani cooked up together.

Mama had been crystal clear about who was to be invited—none of the country club girls or the bridge group. Instead she wanted Scratch and Alyssa, Dell Haley and Fart Unger and Boone Atkins. And Imani, of course.

For some reason, this annoyed the blue blazes out of me. Why usurp my friends, when she had friends of her own? Never mind that they were society snobs and unmitigated idiots. They were still her friends—people like Gladys and Dymple and the two platinum blonde skeletons whose names I could never remember.

But when I brought it up, Mama was adamant. "No," she said. "Assholelutely not." She grinned at the pun and snickered. "Mani's parents, an' Dell, an' Dell's beau—wha's his name?"

"Fart Unger?" I said.

"Yeah." She nodded. "He loves her. I can tell by the way he looks at her."

I was making the list.

"An' that boy who brought you home from the dance." She motioned for me to write it down. "The queer one in the bad suit."

I stared at her. "Boone Atkins?"

"Yeah." She nodded vehemently. "He's your friend, right?"

"Well, yes, but—"

"I wasn't very kind to him," she said.

"Mama, that was years ago. I'm sure he doesn't even remember."

I was sure Boone did remember, because we had talked about it, but I wasn't going to tell Mama that.

"I be nice to him this time."

I patted her hand. "I'm sure you will, Mama. It might be better if you didn't use the word 'queer.'" I went on making the list. "I'll get a lasagna from the deli and make salad and garlic bread. That'll be easy enough."

"No," Mama said.

"What do you mean, no?" I gaped at her.

"Mani likes ham and greens and corn bread."

"Imani can get ham and greens and corn bread every blessed day of the week at the Heartbreak Cafe," I said. "I'm not baking a ham and cooking vegetables from scratch."

In the end, of course, that was exactly what I did. Plus making a homemade banana pudding, which was Imani's favorite dessert.

I might have done the cooking, but even with one hand tied behind her back—or in this case, paralyzed in her lap—Mama was the hostess with the magic touch.

We set up a table outside on the verandah and watched the sun set over the river. Mama told stories about funny things that happened when I was on the pageant circuit, and everybody laughed and had a wonderful time and didn't seem to notice that she slurred her words and drooled now and then.

When the banana pudding was gone and the coffee had been served, Mama dropped her bombshell.

"Tank you for coming," she said. "When Pee and I talked about 'viting some friends for dinner, Pee thought I meant my old friends, the ones I used to have. But they're not my friends anymore. When I had the stroke and got all tristed up and confused, they weren't the ones who came to help me."

She looked around the table. "Fart, you built me a ramp so I could get in and out of the house. You got a funny nickname, but Dell loves you and I can tell you love her, too."

Fart went beet red right to the top of his shiny bald head.

"Dell, you brought me food when Tildy wasn't here. I know you did 'cause Pee's not that great a cook." She grinned at me. "Although she did real good tonight."

Everybody laughed.

"Scratch and Lyssa, you gave me the best gift of all. You let me be GranDonna to this precious child, and she brought me back to life. Again."

Mama wiped a bubble of spittle from the left side of her mouth and went on. "I don't suppose I've been a very nice person during my life," she said. "And I don't deserve having anyone be nice to me now. But sometimes we get more than we deserve. You folks have all been like family to my Pee and cared for her like I couldn't or wouldn't do." She choked up with tears and couldn't go on.

Was this my mother? The woman who never admitted to being wrong about anything? The woman who had given me birth and then spent a lifetime trying to remake me in her own image?

When the doctor said that her inhibitions might be affected, I braced myself for a backlash of nastiness. Not this soft gooey inner core, this outpouring of emotion and mush and candor. I wanted to stop her, to keep her from embarrassing herself.

And me.

But Mama wasn't done.

"Ever'body knows, or at least suspects, that I got money," she was saying. "I dinn't do a thing to earn it 'cept marry Pee's daddy, and most of my life I've spent it on myself. But that's all changed now. You can't wait until you die to tell the people you love how much you love them. By then it's too late. So this is what I'm gonna do. I'm dividing my estate and giving a third of it to each of my children. With one exception: This house and everything in it will belong to Pee."

The scene before me lurched and shifted into slow motion. Mama was giving Belladonna to me? This house, with all its period furnishings, had to be worth a small fortune—maybe even more than the cash value of the estate.

What would Melanie and Harry think? And—the thought shouldered its way rudely to the front of my mind—was this a blessing or a curse?

Mama was still speaking.

"On one condition," she said. "That she'll live here and not sell it."

There it was: the curse wrapped in the blessing.

The shock of it froze me in place. I couldn't move or react. And I wasn't the only one. Around the table, in the gathering dusk, no one stirred or shifted or uttered a single sound.

And meanwhile the second condition went unspoken, hanging out there like a noose swaying in the wind.

On the condition that she'll live here . . . with me.

· 29 ·

"Has she lost her ever-loving mind?" I yelled into the phone. On the other end I could hear Melanie stifling a laugh. "This is not funny," I said.

Melanie took a deep breath and tried to compose herself. "I know."

"Harry's worthless. You're the only one I can talk to," I said. "So what would you do if you were in my place?"

"Well, first of all, I wouldn't be in your place," Melanie said. "Why do you think I moved to California?"

"You did not move halfway across the world to get away from Mama," I said. "You moved because your husband landed a once-in-a-lifetime marketing job at Universal."

"Well, yes, Walton's job was the prime mover, so to

speak. But having a continent between me and Mama was a significant peripheral benefit."

I felt my stomach churn. "Melanie, I can't do this alone."

A long and tense silence stretched between us. "Do you want the house? God knows Harry and I won't fight you for it, if that's what you're worried about. As far as I'm concerned, the whole pile could crumble to rubble, and I wouldn't even show up to watch the bulldozer bury the remains. Mama always loved that house more than she did any of us. When she's gone, you can do whatever you want—sell it, live in it, whatever."

"As long as I stay here and take care of Mama in the meantime. As long as I let you and Harry abdicate your family responsibilities."

"Don't be snotty, Peach. You don't *have* to do anything. You have a choice. We can find a place for her. St. Agnes, maybe. Have you taken over the finances? There should be plenty of money. And if there's not, Walton and I will help. Harry will kick in, too. I'll make sure of that."

She went on talking, spinning out ideas and plans as if somehow the words would help. Finally I couldn't take it anymore. "Mel, shut up."

"What?"

"I said, shut the hell up. I don't need your money, and I don't need your plans. I don't need you to take over and fix this thing. I need you to be a sister."

For a minute or two, she said nothing. Then: "I don't know what you mean."

"Exactly," I said. "And therein lies the problem."

After talking to Melanie, I didn't have the energy to try to contact Harry, who was probably out climbing Kilimanjaro or something. Home for him was Louisville, Kentucky—not an entire continent away, but far enough. He owned a travel agency that catered to the Kentucky blue bloods who bred multimillion-dollar racehorses. Apparently the horsey set spent a lot of their time traveling to exotic places, with my brother as their guide.

Not for the first time, I wondered how the two of them had done so well for themselves when my life seemed like such a mess. And then I thought about Melanie's nervous breakdown after Daddy's death and how Walton hadn't come back with her for the funeral because (Melanie said) he had to meet with the Hollywood brass about some new project. I thought about Harry, the unmarried playboy, who wore his independence like a badge of honor, who laughed too loud and drank too much, and yet beneath the surface seemed like a sad and lonely little boy. I could close my eyes and see him, that day on the back porch when I cracked my skull open, standing over me yelling, "I win! I win!"

He was still winning, but at what cost?

*   *   *

You don't have to do anything. You have a choice.

Melanie's words are still echoing inside my head, the same words I've heard from half a dozen therapists over the years: *You always have a choice. Claim your power to decide.*

I called the old white-haired fool and filled him in on this new wrinkle. He chuckled and said, "Well, isn't that interesting?"

For him, maybe. For me it feels like the manipulation of the century.

And that's the bottom line, isn't it? I'm furious at Mama, furious because I am, to use Dell Haley's word, trapped. I'm angry at the circumstances—at Mama's stroke, at the abdication of my siblings. I'm mad as hell about being left here to deal with this on my own without any help or support.

Anger is what I feel. Rawboned, white-hot fury. But if anger is the manifestation of fear or pain, I need to go underneath the surface and ask myself what I'm afraid of and why I'm so hurt.

The fear is the terror of quicksand, pulling me down so that I'll never get away. That's pretty easy to figure out. The hurt is more difficult. Am I hurt because this is just one more example of Mama trying to control me? Am I hurt because I feel so terribly alone?

Melanie and Harry can throw money at the situation until Judgment Day, and that doesn't give me what I really need. How can I shuffle Mama off to

St. Agnes where some stranger would have to help her settle on the toilet and pull up her panties afterward? I might get furious as blue blazes at her, but I can't just turn my back and walk away.

I was all set to go, to leave Chulahatchie and get my life back. Now lightning has struck, and I'm that single tree standing out in the middle of nowhere, split down the middle and smoldering.

"Why?" I said. It was the question I'd been asking myself ever since Mama dropped her bombshell at dinner on Saturday night. Now I was asking Dell.

"I don't know," Dell said. "Maybe she's scared, Peach. Your mama's always been fiercely independent and capable."

I gave her my best sarcastic grimace. "You think?"

Dell didn't take the bait. Instead she just smiled and went on talking. "Now she's had the stroke, and her whole life has changed. She's lost her identity. She's lost her freedom. She's drowning."

"And she wants to take me down with her?"

"I doubt that she has any truly evil purpose in mind. I expect she's just scared."

"Well, so am I."

Dell gave me an intent look. "What are you afraid of?"

I thought about this for a minute. "All my life, Dell, I've been tangled up in my mother's plans for me. She was determined to bring me up as a Southern Lady. Soybean

Queen, Miss Ole Miss, all of it. For God's sake, she had me fitted for the Miss America crown by the time I was six. And when it didn't happen, when I disappointed her, there was hell to pay."

I took a sip of my coffee and toyed with the slice of fudge pie in front of me. "And I *always* disappointed her, Dell. Always. It was never enough. All I ever wanted was for her to be proud of me. Of me. Not of what I did or accomplished or won, but of me. Just me, myself. Proud of the person I turned out to be."

"Are *you* proud of you?" Dell asked.

"Excuse me?"

"Are you proud of yourself?" she repeated. "Do you like who you are, the person you've become? Are you enough for yourself?"

"Well, yes," I said. "For the most part. I mean, I'm not proud of some of the things I've done, but I've grown a lot in the past year. I feel more centered, more comfortable in my own skin." I reached out and touched her hand, just lightly, then pulled away. "I've got friends."

"Then does it really matter what your mother thinks?"

We sat in silence with the question hanging between us. After a minute Dell got up, gave me a quick kiss on the top of the head, and squeezed my shoulder.

"If you really want to understand why your mama did this," she said, "I'd suggest asking the only one who knows."

The whole world, it seemed, was blooming on Mother's Day.

I got Mama up, fixed her hair, and helped her dress, and together we went to church. The minister preached, predictably, about the high and holy calling of motherhood and all the sacrifices mothers made for their children. The Gospel according to Hallmark.

The old anger stirred in me again. I wondered briefly if church was supposed to leave you mad and seething. This time, however, the anger was not directed at Mama but at a society that led us to believe in this kind of unattainable perfection.

My mind drifted, and what surfaced in the mix of

random thoughts was a vivid recollection of the bad poetry
I'd shuffled through at the card store two days earlier:

Mom, You've Always Been There for Me.

Nope.

A Mother's Love Is Forever.

Not exactly.

Mother, I Hope I Turn Out Just Like You.

Lord, deliver me.

I ventured a sidelong glance at Mama. She appeared
to be listening intently and drooling just a little on the left
side. I took a tissue out of my purse and dabbed at her
chin. She turned and looked at me.

She wasn't drooling. She was crying.

Back at home I got Mama out of her church clothes and
into her housedress, and I was about to go warm up leftovers for our lunch when she stopped me.

"Hep," she said.

I turned to see her holding out the Mother's Day cor-
sage the church had provided for all the mothers. It was
rather pathetic, really, a couple of carnations dyed lavender and held together with florist tape. But she wanted it,
so I pinned it to her dress, where it clashed mightily with
the blue and pink stripes.

"Let me change clothes," I said, "and then I'll fix us
some lunch."

"Take a time," Mama said. "I be onna perch."

I smiled to myself. For over thirty years, ever since Daddy bought and renovated Belladonna for her, Mama had steadfastly refused to use the word "porch" and instantly corrected anyone who dared to utter the word in her presence. Verandah, she said. It was a verandah, not a porch.

Poor people, I suppose, had porches. Only the privileged few had verandahs.

With the stroke, our back verandah had been demoted. It was now the porch, the reading room, the dining space, the place for Mama to sit and watch the world go by.

And today the world was putting on quite a show.

Down the lawn the azaleas were still in high bloom— hot pink, pale pink, and fuchsia; lavender and white and dark purple. A curving swath of color punctuated by an occasional splash of yellow. Clumps of bluestar and butterfly bushes, red-hot pokers and bright yellow sedum.

I came out and sat beside her, following her gaze out toward the river, breathing in the mixed perfumes of grass and flower and fresh spring breeze. When I let my eyes unfocus, the colors mingled and swam before me like the Christmas lights, like a gift unwrapping itself layer by layer.

"Beauty-full, inn't it?" Mama said.

"Yes," I said.

And it was. I felt as if I were seeing spring for the first time, the loveliness of Belladonna, the quiet of the early afternoon. As if it had been there all along, but hidden behind a veil of painful memories.

I thought about Dell's advice, that if I wanted answers, I should go to the only one who held them. "Mama," I said, "why did you decide to leave Belladonna to me? And why the condition that I had to live here?"

"Dahlin'," she said, "inn't it obvious?"

"Not to me," I said. I wanted to add, *Unless your purpose is to blackmail me into staying here against my will.* But something stopped me. Some look in her eyes—a look I had never seen before, or if I had seen it, I hadn't recognized or acknowledged it.

Love.

"You are my chile," she said. "My younges', my daughter, my baby. I try to bring you up right, to teach you ever'thing I knew. I dinn't do such a good job. But you grown up real good, and now I'm old, and it's your turn."

She bit her lip and blinked back the tears that were almost always with her now, at the first sign of any emotion. "Nobody wans to have a shroke," she went on, "but there's always a blessin' on the backside of the curse."

I stared at her, waiting. This was my mother, talking about blessings and curses, opening a vein, revealing herself with such vulnerability? I didn't dare speak or move, and besides that, I had nothing to say.

"The blessin'," she said, "is insight." She paused and rubbed at her paralyzed left hand. "I always cared too much about appearances, about what other people thought. People like Gaddie an' that biscuit-dough lump of a daughter of hers."

I tried unsuccessfully to hide the grin, but Mama saw it and smiled, too, ducking her head the way Imani did when she was feeling shy or embarrassed. "But look a' me now. I got all the external stuff stripped away, and this is what I'm left with." She lifted her left claw and waved it awkwardly.

I opened my mouth to protest, but she shot me a look that shut me right up. "I got eyes," she said. "I can see. And this is what I've learned from being trapped in here: What's important is what's on the inside. In the heart. In the soul."

She fixed her one good eye on me. "You wanna know why I lef' Belladonna to you?" she asked. "It's because I don't have anythin' else to give you. I've watched you this year. You got a good heart. You got friends who love you. You been kind to me when God knows I didn't give you any reason to. You dinn't abandon me when I got sick."

"Oh, Mama, I couldn't have—"

She held up her hand for silence and turned her face out toward the river. "Look at this place," she said. "It's peaceful and beautiful, and—" She paused and took a breath. "It's yours. It's the kind of place a writer ought to have."

I frowned at her. "A writer?"

" 'Course," she said. "Ever'body knows that's what you want to do. Mani told me. Dell told me. Your queer friend Boone told me."

"Gay," I said.

She ignored this. "It's all you ever do, write in that journal of yours."

I didn't bother telling her that journaling was a kind of therapy for me, that if she read what I'd written about her, it'd curl her hair so tight she'd never need to get a perm again. I didn't tell her how much I dreaded the idea of living in this house and taking care of her for the rest of her life.

Instead I said, "But Mama, Chulahatchie's not my home."

"Home is where you're loved," she said. "Home is where people accept you for who you are." She gave a one-sided shrug. "No wonder you never felt at home here."

It was the closest she ever got to admitting the truth about our relationship as mother and daughter. Before the tears overtook her, she rushed ahead. "You got friends here, folks who love you and need you. Family, like Dell and Boone and Imani. If you don't feel quite at home, then just visit for a while longer. Give yourself time to write that book that's been stewing around inside your head."

I knew what my answer had to be. I'd known it even before we started this conversation, but that didn't make it any easier. All the heaviness in my heart came out on a sigh.

"All right, Mama. I'll stay."

I have to admit, she's right about one thing. I do have people here who love me—love me enough to forgive me when I screw up, love me enough not to hold my woundedness against me. It's more than I could say for the place I once called "home." All I have there is an ex-husband who traded me in on a younger model and—if the lack of communication is any indication—took all our mutual friends along with him.

I'm staying in Chulahatchie for the time being, not because Mama has signed over Belladonna to me but because it's the right thing to do. At the moment my motivation is eighty percent duty and twenty percent love, but I have hopes that in time I'll arrive at the tipping point where love moves up front and center and duty takes a backseat.

Still, duty's not such a bad motive where mothers and daughters are concerned. I never thought about it from that point of view, but maybe being a mother is sometimes eighty percent duty and twenty percent love, as well. And if Mama did the best she could with me, well, then, I guess I'll just do the best I can with her.

I told my therapist everything, and he asked the one question I hadn't thought of: Does it really matter what the motive is? Doesn't it matter more that you do the right thing and let the feelings sort themselves out in their own time?

Maybe the old fool really is worth eighty bucks an hour.

I'm still working on it, this business of letting the

emotions sort themselves out. I'm not so good at being patient. Not so good at waiting, at holding life with an open hand.

It's the Buddhist way, Boone tells me: centering myself in my truth, letting go of outcomes, trusting the universe to bring things right. A Catholic Buddhist— now, that seems like a pretty significant oxymoron, but then Boone's always danced to his own rhythms.

"Pee?"

I looked up as my mother shuffled out onto the back verandah, leaning on her walker. "Hey, Mama."

"I dinn't mean to interrupt you."

"It's okay, Mama. I'm just journaling."

She sat down with a thud in the chair next to me, reached out with her good hand, and began stroking my fingers. "I talk to Jane Lee Custer at St. Agnes," she said. "They got a studio apartment available; I can move in next week."

I might have had a minor TIA of my own; her words went right past me like an echo in a dark chamber. "What are you talking about, Mama? What do you mean, move?"

She gazed at me with the softest expression I'd ever seen on her face. Even ravaged and lopsided, she had never looked more beautiful. "Honey, I dinn't give you Bella-donna so you could nurse me. You got other things to do.

Important things. You dinn't think I was gonna live here with you and expect you to take care of me?"

"Well, yes, I thought you were going to stay," I said. "I thought that was the whole point."

"The whole point?" Her expression shifted from tenderness to inexpressible sadness. "You thought I gave you Belladonna in exchange for—"

She shook her head. "It was a gift, honey. Always a gift. Never a bribe."

Epilogue

As the old white-haired fool is fond of saying, some-times progress moves along at glacial speed, and some-times it takes quantum leaps forward. I looked into my mother's eyes, and in that moment love woke up, took off, and left duty in the dust.

"Stay, Mama," I said. "I want you to stay here with me. Whatever we have to work out, we'll work out together."

Melanie was sure I'd had a nervous breakdown of my own. But then my sister can't see our mother sitting here in her blue striped housedress and no makeup, watching the sun go down over the river. She can't un-derstand how the evening light sets Mama's white hair aflame with the auburn tints of her girlhood or illuminates her face like candlelight or turns that one bubble of spittle into a diamond on her lip.

I'm not claiming it'll stay that way. I'm sure there'll be times I'll want to wring her neck and probably times she'd like to kill me, too, if she had two good hands. But I meant what I said about wanting her to stay. I meant it with all my heart.

I still mean it.

Like everyone else in this world, I'm just doing the best I can.